From the Na

THE CASE: Find out who's responsible for the deadly accidents to George during an international bike racing competition.

CONTACT: Steven Lloyd—*handsome young owner of a successful computer company and George's racing sponsor.*

SUSPECTS: Tatyana Ivanova—*the Russian champion being controlled by the KGB.*

Debbi Howe—*she's terribly jealous of George's romance with her former fiancé.*

Monique Vandervoort—*the Dutch entrant who is determined to win at any cost.*

COMPLICATIONS: George's romance with Jon seems to be on the rocks. Then Steven Lloyd's new software is stolen and held for ransom. The thief wants Nancy to deliver the money. Can she handle two cases at once?

Nancy Drew Files™ available in Armada

1 Secrets Can Kill
2 Deadly Intent
3 Murder on Ice
4 Smile and Say Murder
5 Hit-and-Run Holiday
6 White Water Terror
7 Deadly Doubles
8 Two Points to Murder
9 False Moves
10 Buried Secrets
11 Heart of Danger
12 Fatal Ransom
13 Wings of Fear
14 This Side of Evil
15 Trial by Fire
16 Never Say Die
17 Stay Tuned for Danger
18 Circle of Evil
19 Sisters in Crime
20 Very Deadly Yours

THE NANCY DREW FILES™

Case 16

Never Say Die

Carolyn Keene

ARMADA

First published in the USA in 1988 by
Simon & Schuster Inc.
First published in Great Britain
in Armada in 1991
This impression 1991

Armada is an imprint of
HarperCollins Children's Books,
part of HarperCollins Publishers Ltd,
77–85 Fulham Palace Road,
Hammersmith, London W6 8JB

Printed and bound in Great Britain by
HarperCollins Manufacturing, Glasgow

Chapter One

SHADING HER EYES with her hand, Nancy Drew stood in the middle of the Summitville Velodrome and turned in a circle. Around her, junior cyclists from all over the world were practicing on the outdoor concrete track, which had just been built in a small town near River Heights.

"All right! Look at them go!" said Ned Nickerson, her boyfriend, who was standing next to her. "What do you think, Nancy?"

"Umm," Nancy mumbled.

"Ned, how can you sound so excited?" Nancy's friend Bess Marvin asked. "Track cycling is terrifying. Right, Nan?"

"Umm," she said.

Ned chuckled. "Hey, Nancy, aren't you listening to us?"

"Huh?" Nancy asked, suddenly turning toward him.

"I said—oh, never mind. What's got into you? You've been off in the ozone ever since we got here."

"Sorry," Nancy said. "I guess my mind was on other things."

"Like what? A new case?"

Smiling, Nancy shook her head. Being an amateur private detective kept her pretty busy, so it was a natural assumption for him to make.

"No, it's something else," she said, turning back to the track.

The truth was, she was thinking about one of the cyclists. Squinting against the bright summer sun, she scanned the track—there! The rider was just speeding into a steeply banked turn.

"Nancy . . ." Ned said persistently.

"Oh, I'm sorry," Nancy answered. "I'm just worried, that's all."

"About what?" Bess asked curiously. As she turned to look at her friend, a strand of her long straw-blond hair fell forward over her right shoulder.

Before Nancy could reply, the rider she was watching swung off the track and headed toward them. She slowed down and was finally stopped a few feet from Nancy by a tall blond boy. He had a clipboard in one hand, and a stopwatch dangled from his neck.

"Bummer," Nancy heard George Fayne remark, as she looked at the time on the watch with a scowl. "I'm probably the slowest rider out there."

"No, you're not," said Jon Berntsen, her boyfriend and coach. "Far from it."

"Well, I feel slow. Check out all those disk-wheel bikes, Jon! Mine's an antique compared to them. I'm not going to win one single event," she moaned.

Nancy frowned. George was obsessed with winning every event in the Summitville Junior Classic. But why?

George had always been competitive. She was more dedicated to sports than anyone Nancy knew. But ever since George had taken up cycling a few months before, it was as if she had become a machine. She trained constantly. She was pushing herself to the limit—and probably beyond. What was George trying to prove? Nancy wondered.

"George, are those bikes really faster than yours?" Nancy asked, walking the few steps over to her friend.

"You bet," George answered. "They're a lot more aerodynamic."

"Because the wheels have those disks instead of spokes?"

"Uh-huh. And also because of the way they're designed. See how they slope forward? The front wheel is smaller. Well, that angles you lower, so your back is flatter. You create less resistance to the wind."

"I get it," Nancy said, nodding. That made sense.

But it wasn't fair. If the other girls had better equipment, that meant they had an advantage over George. Nancy couldn't blame George for being upset—especially after all the training she had done.

"If only I had enough money," George said, climbing off her old spoke-wheel model. "I'd love to buy a disk-wheel bike."

"What about the money you earned?" Bess asked her cousin.

"It's gone. And anyway, it wouldn't have been enough. Those things are expensive."

Ned frowned. "What about your sponsor? Why don't you ask him to get you one?"

"Steven Lloyd? I couldn't," George answered.

"Why not?"

"Because he's already done so much. I mean, aside from building this velodrome in the first place, he paid for my skin suit, my entry fee —even Jon's coaching."

Nancy understood George's feelings. It was hard to ask for favors when someone had already been very generous. Of course, Steven Lloyd could afford to buy a hundred disk-wheel bikes if he wanted them. His software company was a huge success. Still, whether to ask was George's decision. Nancy wasn't going to interfere.

At least George had Jon, Nancy thought. He was the perfect coach for her. He was an experienced athlete—a former Olympic skier—so he not only knew how to win, but he knew how to handle setbacks, too.

Thinking back, Nancy remembered the ski vacation on which George and Jon had first met. Back then, Jon had not been the easygoing guy he was now. He had been withdrawn and bitter, believing himself to be responsible for the death of another skier. But Nancy had proved that it wasn't true in a case she privately called *Murder on Ice.* Now Jon was much happier and more optimistic.

"Speaking of your sponsor, here he is!" Jon said just then.

Nancy's attention snapped back to the group as she saw a handsome, sandy-haired man in his late twenties walking up to them. Nancy knew Steven Lloyd because he was a client of her father's law firm.

Another man was with him. He was tall—even taller than Ned—with red hair and dark green eyes. Nancy didn't know him, but because of the suit he was wearing she guessed that he was an associate of Steven Lloyd's. He was carrying a disk-wheel bike, which he set down carefully when they reached the group.

"Hello, George. Hi, everyone." Steven nodded toward the other man. "This is my executive assistant, Peter Cooper."

"Please call me Peter," he said, smiling.

When the introductions were through, Steven patted the bike's seat. "Well, George, what do you think?"

"It's gorgeous," she said enviously. "It's a Bussetti, isn't it?"

"Sure is. One of the finest track bikes made."

"I'd love to have one like that." George sighed.

"You do."

"What?"

Steven smiled. "It's yours for the duration of the Classic. I had it flown over from Europe by air express."

"You're kidding!"

"I'm serious. Why don't you try it out?"

George didn't have to be asked twice. Thanking Steven profusely, she took the bike from Peter and wheeled it out to the track's apron. A moment later she was off, moving slowly at first, then gaining momentum from the heavy disk wheels.

Nancy was amazed. By the first turn George was moving very fast. By the second she was practically flying.

"Amazing," Ned said, shaking his head. "You wouldn't think disk wheels would make that much of a difference."

Steven shrugged. "They do, there's the proof.

You know," he said, "I think we're looking at the next World Junior Champion."

"George is lucky to have such a generous sponsor," Ned said.

"She deserves the best," Steven said. "I was just afraid the bike wouldn't get here in time."

"Was there a shipping problem?" Nancy asked.

"Yes. In fact, we couldn't get it through customs until late last night."

"Last night! That's cutting it a little close, isn't it?"

"You're not kidding," Steven said with a laugh. "And that was only the beginning. Once we got it, we discovered that it wasn't assembled."

"You mean you put it together yourself?"

"Not me. Peter did," Steven explained. "He spent all night in my office with his cycling tools."

"I guess you're interested in cycling," Nancy said, turning to Peter.

He didn't reply. His eyes were fixed on the track.

"Peter?" Nancy repeated.

"Hmm. Oh, I've been cycling most of my life," Peter said, abruptly turning back to the group. "Mostly road cycling, though," he added, his eyes drifting back to the track. He was watching George, Nancy realized.

A few minutes later George slowed down and

pulled into the infield. Everyone crowded around to congratulate her.

"This bike is terrific," George declared. "There's just one problem—the seat's too low. It needs to be raised a few inches."

"No problem," Peter said, springing forward. "I'll just take the bike out to the parking lot. The tools are in my car."

Jon pulled a wrench from his pocket. "Don't bother. I'll get it."

"It's no trouble. Really. Here, let me have it—" Peter started to take the bike, but Jon held on.

"This will only take a second—see?" he said. In a flash he had loosened the seat post. Raising the seat, he clamped the bolt down again. "There. All done."

George climbed back on, and moments later she returned to the track to continue warming up. Everyone looked happy—everyone but Peter, Nancy noticed. He was scowling.

Steven turned to his assistant. "Is the official time clock working yet?"

"I'm not sure. I'll get right on it."

"I've given Peter a leave of absence from the office so he can run the Classic for me," Steven explained.

"Yes, you'll be seeing a lot of me in the next six days," Peter said. "Along with my other duties, I'm trying to line up some interviews for George and the other contestants."

"You are? Fantastic!" Bess exclaimed.

"Publicity for George and the others is publicity for the company," he said smoothly. "Well, I guess I'd better see about the official clock." He turned and left.

Steven left a minute later as the officials began to clear the track for the first event—the qualifying round of the Women's 3,000-Meter Individual Pursuit.

George was scheduled for the third heat. The race was similar to a chase, except that the two riders started on opposite sides of the track. If one caught the other, she won. If neither got caught, the winner was the one who rode three thousand meters in the fastest time.

Nancy's heart was pounding as George waited on the back straightaway for her start. Pursuit was a brutal event, and George's opponent looked strong.

"Ladies, attention!" an official called over the loudspeaker. A second later the starting pistol fired. They were off.

"Go, George!" Nancy shouted.

"Come on, Fayne!" Bess hollered.

The other girl shot forward. She was a strong rider, and by the end of the first lap she was a second and a half ahead. But her lead didn't last. Slowly but surely, George began to whittle it down.

"Come on, George!" Ned yelled.

"Go, George!" Bess roared.

With just three laps to go, George moved ahead. Her opponent put on a burst of speed to try to catch up, but George was faster. As she finished, Nancy let out a whoop. George had won!

Well-wishers crowded around as George steered off the track. Beaming, she whipped off her teardrop-shaped helmet and tossed it to Bess.

"All riiight!" Jon gave George a quick hug.

But not everyone was excited about George's victory. As Nancy scanned the crowd, she noticed a girl with close-cropped white-blond hair who was wearing an orange jersey. She was glaring at George with hatred in her eyes.

"Who's that?" Nancy asked Jon in a whisper, nodding toward the girl.

He glanced over. "Who? Oh, that's Monique Vandervoort, from Holland."

"What do you know about her? She sure doesn't look too friendly."

"She's the current World Junior Champion. She also held the record in this event. George just broke it."

Nancy nodded. That explained it. Monique had some hot new competition, and she probably didn't like it one bit.

A moment later the Dutch girl spun around and stalked toward the exit tunnel that ran under the track to the outside. Nancy turned to George, who was bubbling enthusiastically about her new bike.

"Nothing's going to stop me now. Except maybe this heat. Anyone want anything to drink?" she asked, handing her bike to Jon. "I'm going to get something."

No one else was thirsty. Shrugging, George walked toward the exit tunnel. A minute later she was out of the velodrome and out of sight.

Nancy turned back to watch the next heat. When it was over, the spectators applauded, and another heat began. Nancy was beginning to wonder what was keeping George. Surely it didn't take this long to get a drink.

Just then Ned grabbed her arm. "Nancy, where's that smoke coming from?"

"Smoke?" Glancing around, she saw the cloud of thick black smoke rising outside, just behind the stands. At the same moment she heard someone shout, "Fire! There's a fire!"

George! Was she all right? All at once a sick feeling hit Nancy in the stomach. Without a word, she broke into a run.

Chapter Two

NANCY WAS THE first person to reach the tent where refreshments were being sold. The tent had collapsed, and one side was in flames. From inside a hysterical voice was screaming for help.

George!

"Hold on, I'm coming!" Nancy shouted.

Wildly, she glanced around. Where was everyone? she wondered. What had happened to the security guards she'd noticed when they arrived? Why weren't they nearby?

But she didn't have time to worry. Lifting the canvas, she found the entrance flap, ducked under, and began to push toward George's voice.

She moved forward slowly, holding the heavy material up with her hands.

It was tough going—and very smoky. Finally, though, Nancy found George. She was near the middle of the tent, doubled over and coughing.

"George, quick! Follow me!"

Spinning around, Nancy turned back toward the entrance flap. But the canvas between her and it was now a sea of orange-red flames. Desperately, she grabbed George's hand, and the two girls began to push in another direction toward the tent's outer wall.

But when they finally reached the edge, it was staked down tightly. Nancy and George grabbed the heavy cloth and heaved upward with all their might. A gap appeared. George dove through first, still coughing. Nancy dropped to the ground, lifted the canvas, and rolled out, too. She needed fresh air—fast!

"Nancy!"

Ned swept her up in his arms and began to run with her. She clung to him gratefully, but it wasn't until they were far away from the smoke that she finally felt safe.

"Thanks," she whispered, her heart hammering as he set her down.

"Anytime," Ned answered tightly. There was anger in his eyes—he hated it when she risked her life—but there was pride there, too.

Nancy ran her hand through her hair and

looked around. George was sitting nearby with Jon. "What happened?" Nancy asked.

George shook her head and coughed. "I don't know. I was waiting for my drink, when all of a sudden the tent came down on top of me. Then I smelled smoke and started to yell."

"Was anyone else in there?" Nancy asked, glancing back toward the fire.

"No. A couple of race officials were in there getting sandwiches, but they left. There was a woman handing out sodas, too, but she went out to get some ice."

"Thank goodness," Nancy said, wiping her forehead on the sleeve of her shirt. "At least no one was hurt."

The tent was now completely wrapped in flames. People were tossing buckets of water on it, but Nancy could see that it was hopeless. Clouds of thick black smoke billowed up into the sunny summer sky.

For a moment she just watched the spectacle. A large crowd was forming as cyclists and coaches poured from the exit tunnel. Then she turned back to George. "How are you feeling?"

"I'm fine now," George replied. She was on her feet and no longer coughing. "Thanks for going in to get me."

"Yes, you saved her life," Jon added.

"All in a day's work," Nancy said, joking. Her tone was light, but her heart was not. That sure was a close one.

Suddenly a panicky look crossed George's face. "My bike!"

Ned shook his head in disbelief. "George, you're amazing. You almost got killed a minute ago."

"I know," she said, "but I just want to make sure the bike's all right."

"Don't worry. Bess is inside guarding it," he told her, shaking his head.

That's George, Nancy thought. Only George would worry more about a bike than about herself.

The sound of sirens interrupted her thoughts. The Summitville Fire Department had just arrived. Spotting the chief, she went over and reported all she had seen. When she was through, she suggested that he list the fire's cause as "suspicious."

"Too soon to say what it was," the chief barked in response. "Could have been anything. A cigarette, maybe."

"I doubt that," Nancy replied. "Cigarette fires smolder before they burn. This one spread very quickly."

"Did you see it start?" the chief asked, studying her.

"No, but my friend was inside the tent. She said everything was fine until it collapsed."

"The fire must have burned through the support ropes, causing the collapse," the chief said.

"No, you don't understand. She said the tent fell down, and *then* the fire started."

The chief glared at her. "Are you saying it was arson?"

"I don't know. But I believe the fire could have been set deliberately," Nancy said.

"Young lady, arson is a serious crime," the chief said, raising his eyebrows. "I wouldn't go around even speculating unless I were—"

"Excuse me, Chief." A fireman wearing a grave expression broke in. "I thought you'd like to see this. We found it stashed in that garbage can over there."

He held out a five-gallon gasoline can, the type motorists carry for emergencies. The chief shook it. It was empty.

"Hmm. Looks like you may have been right after all," the chief told Nancy. "By the way, what's your name?"

"Nancy Drew."

"Hmm. Mine's Mike McShane. Well, let's have a look around, shall we?"

Together Nancy and Chief McShane walked around the charred remains of the tent, which was lying soaked with water. At first Nancy saw nothing, but then suddenly she stopped.

"Chief, look at the support ropes. The ones on the other side of the tent are still tied to their stakes."

"So?"

"The ones on the opposite side aren't. The knots are untied."

The chief peered down at the stakes. "You're right," he said. "Someone did untie them."

"That explains how the tent collapsed."

What it didn't explain, of course, was who had set the fire. Or why. Nancy examined the wreckage for any further clue but found none. She looked at the gas can, but it was made of rough plastic. Lifting fingerprints would be impossible. Nancy knew she was stuck. Anyone could be responsible for the fire, anyone at all.

After saying goodbye to the chief, she went back into the velodrome. George was pulling on her warm-up jacket, getting ready to go home.

"Any news?" Ned asked Nancy then.

Nancy told the group what she had discovered. "The question," she said, concluding, "is why? Who would want to burn down the tent?"

"Someone trying to sabotage the Classic," Bess said.

"Or maybe someone trying to hurt Steven Lloyd," Ned said.

Jon looked grim. "Well, I don't agree. I think it was someone who was trying to hurt George. Maybe even kill her."

"But why?" Nancy asked.

"To knock her out of the competition."

"Another cyclist, you mean?" Nancy looked doubtful. "I don't know. Do you really think it's possible that anyone could want to win that badly?"

"It's possible. Anything's possible," Jon said.

"We'd better play it safe and keep a close eye on George," Nancy said.

"It wouldn't hurt," the others said.

"No, it wouldn't—look!" George exclaimed. In her hand was a note she had just pulled from the pocket of her windbreaker.

Nancy took it. The message was spelled out in letters cut from a magazine.

"What does it say?" Ned asked.

Nancy read it in a flat, steady voice: " 'Quit the Classic, or else.' "

A few minutes later George had loaded her new bike into the rear of her family's station wagon and left.

"I'm going to follow her in my car and make sure she gets home all right," Nancy told the others.

"Want me to go with you?" Ned offered. "Or maybe Bess?"

"No, I can handle it alone," Nancy said. "You stay and watch the racing."

The others had driven to the velodrome in their own cars, so Nancy knew she would not have to return. As she was leaving, Jon pulled her aside. He had to stay behind to register George for a race later that evening, but he was still concerned about the note she had found in her pocket.

"Don't worry," Nancy told him. "It probably isn't connected to the fire."

"How can you be sure?"

"I can't. But if someone really intended for George to be asphyxiated in the tent, why would they bother to hide a warning note in her windbreaker? She'd never see it!"

"Maybe it was put there after you rescued her."

"Well, I suppose that's possible," Nancy said slowly. "But we can't draw any conclusions. Not yet, anyway."

"So what do we do—wait for something worse to happen?"

"At the moment it's our only option. But don't worry. I doubt anything worse will happen."

Nancy's Mustang was parked in the lot reserved for competitors and their crews. As she started the engine and backed out of her space, she thought about Monique Vandervoort, the cyclist who had been glaring at George. Could she have set the fire? She had left the stadium right before George, Nancy remembered, but that proved nothing. How would she know George would follow?

Several minutes later Nancy pulled into the parking lot of a large motel called the Imperial. It was close to the velodrome, so most of the cyclists from out of town were staying there. George had pulled in just a minute or two before Nancy. She had wanted to meet some of the other cyclists and cool off with a swim in the motel pool.

The motel's courtyard was all but deserted. Nancy looked around and spotted George walking up to the pool. She stopped to greet a girl with short dark hair, large dark eyes, and the unmistakable muscular legs of a trained cyclist.

Nancy didn't want to butt in on their conversation, so she slowly locked her car. As she started moving toward the pool, she noticed that two more people had joined George and the dark girl. One was a lean, powerful-looking man with curly black hair. The other was a tiny woman in her thirties who had a square-shaped face.

The woman was speaking sharply to George's companion. Nancy was still too far away to hear what she was saying, but it was obvious from the girl's expression that she was upset.

Suddenly the girl stood up, snatched her towel, and marched angrily into the motel. The older couple followed and were trailed in turn by George, who seemed to be speaking to them in a raised voice.

Curious, Nancy walked toward the group. Before she reached them, though, the girl had disappeared inside her room. George continued her argument with the adults, but they cut it short by going inside, too. The door was slammed in George's face.

"What's going on?" Nancy asked, walking up to her friend. "Who was that girl?"

"Hi, Nancy. That was Tatyana Ivanova," George replied. "She's from the Soviet Union."

"What was all the fuss about?"

"Did you see those two people with her?"

"Uh-huh. Who are they?"

Taking Nancy by the elbow, George led her away from Tatyana's door. "They call themselves her chaperons, but Tatyana told me they're actually KGB!"

Just then, Tatyana's door snapped open. The muscular man walked out. Without looking at George or Nancy, he started back toward the pool. Nancy turned to George.

"The KGB!" she whispered. "Are you sure you heard right?"

"Yes. Tatyana told me they don't want her to have any contact with Westerners. Can you believe it?" George said.

"I suppose so. I think they treat all their visiting athletes and artists that way."

"It's crazy," George said hotly.

"I know. It's hard for us to understand, but they see us as a threat."

George said nothing, but Nancy could see that she was fuming. She didn't really blame her. At the same time, though, she hoped that George would accept the situation. Further contact might get Tatyana in trouble.

Slowly the two girls walked out, passing the pool. On the way, they saw the muscular man, who was returning to Tatyana's room with a pair of sunglasses in his hand.

"Did you see that?" George whispered when he was out of earshot. "She left her sunglasses by the pool, and they wouldn't even let her go back to get them herself."

A minute later Nancy pushed open the gate to the pool. "Ready to go?"

"In a minute. I want to take a quick dip," George said. "I hope the owners won't mind."

"There's no one here. I don't think they'll care. I'll wait right here for you."

Dropping into a chair, Nancy watched as George mounted the diving board and positioned herself for a dive. She slowly raised her arms as she began her approach.

Just then, Nancy noticed a cord trailing into the water. At the end of it was a radio—and it was plugged into an all-weather socket on the side of the cabana!

Nancy leaped up. "George, don't dive!" she screamed.

But it was too late. As she yelled, George bounced off the board and went soaring into the air!

Chapter Three

NANCY TENSED. HORRIFIED, she watched as George sliced into the water. Her form was perfect, but there was just one problem—the pool was probably electrified!

In no time, Nancy was at the water's edge. Come on, George! Come up for air! she screamed mentally. Come up! Come up!

But George didn't come up. Beneath the water's wavery surface, Nancy saw her friend frog-kicking toward the aluminum ladder.

"Oh no!"

There was no time to lose. If George touched that ladder she'd be electrocuted instantly. Taking a deep breath, Nancy dove into the water fully clothed.

The water was cold, and her water-soaked clothes weighed her down, but Nancy barely noticed either. She swam furiously. When she reached George, she grabbed her friend's ankle. Sputtering, they both surfaced at the same time.

"Nancy! What are you doing?"

"George, don't touch that!" Nancy caught her friend's hand as she reached for the ladder. "It could kill you!"

"Wow, you must have had too many hot dogs for lunch," George said with a laugh. "What are you talking about?"

Treading water, Nancy explained the situation. George's eyes went wide when she saw the radio dangling into the pool.

Then she chuckled. "Nan, you dope. Don't you remember anything from physics class? When that radio fell in the water, it shorted a fuse. We're not in any danger."

"Oh really?" Nancy said. "What if the fuse *didn't* blow? Do you want to take that chance?"

George eyed the ladder uncertainly. "Well—I guess not."

"Neither do I. Especially not after what happened back at the velodrome. We've got to figure out a way to get out of here."

Nancy looked around. There was no one who could help them. For a moment she considered simply hauling herself out of the water without the ladder, but then she decided against it. If there was a puddle on the walk around the pool that made a connection with the ground—zap! She'd be instant boiled detective.

Then she hit upon a solution. It was simple, but would it work?

"Where are you going?" George asked.

Nancy swam toward the radio. "To get us out of here, I hope!"

As she got closer, she saw that the cord ran straight from the radio to an outdoor socket on the cabana. Reaching over, Nancy grasped the cord and gave it a sharp yank. A moment later the plug popped out of the socket.

"Phew! All clear, George. We can even use the ladder now."

Once she was out of the pool, Nancy grabbed George's towel and immediately darted inside the cabana. She was searching for a fuse box. It was near the door. Just as she'd suspected, the fuse had been taken out and dropped on the floor. A copper penny was in its place.

"See, what did I tell you?" she said as George came in. "If you had touched that ladder, you'd be dead right now."

George sighed. "That's the second time today you've saved me from disaster. Thanks."

"Forget it."

George didn't mention the incident again, but Nancy kept thinking about it. As she patted herself dry with the towel, she tried to reason it through. Who was responsible? And why had they done it?

The most obvious suspect was the KGB agent who had carried Tatyana's sunglasses back from the pool. He had had the opportunity. And he had a motive—to keep George from talking to Tatyana.

But Nancy didn't buy that explanation. For one thing, murder was too extreme a solution for the KGB's problem. For another, the KGB agent wasn't the only one who had had the opportunity. While she and George were talking near Tatyana's door, anyone could have set the trap.

It was even possible that it was an accident. A motel employee could have put the penny in the fuse box days—even weeks—before. Then, a passerby could have knocked the radio into the pool without being aware of it.

Maybe. Nancy glanced around. There was no one in sight—not even a maid. Then she saw something. Across the courtyard, at a window on the second story, there was movement! The curtains were slowly being pulled closed.

Shading her eyes, Nancy strained to see. The window was pretty far away, but she could just make out the figure of a girl in the center of the window before the drapes were drawn all the way. The girl had close-cropped white-blond hair.

It was Monique Vandervoort! How badly did

the Dutch girl want to stay on top? Nancy wondered. Badly enough to electrify a pool?

Nancy knew she would simply have to gather more evidence. And that might mean waiting for another attempt on George's life.

That night Nancy returned to the velodrome and stood with Ned and Bess in the infield to watch George compete. It was a warm evening, and a large crowd was in the stands. Excitement built as the racing progressed, but Nancy's mind was elsewhere.

She felt edgy. Unsettled. Would there be another attack on George? she wondered. And if so, when? And how? She didn't know the answers, of course, but she did know one thing—if it happened, she wanted to be there!

For her part, George didn't seem all that concerned about what might happen. As she waited for the start of her event, she wandered around the infield, chatting easily with the other cyclists. How could she remain so cool? Nancy wondered. Didn't she realize that she might be in danger?

Finally, George's event began. It was the first round of the Women's Match Sprint.

"Both riders start together on the home straight," Jon explained. "They circle the track three times, going slowly, then they sprint the last two hundred meters. Whoever wins the sprint wins the ride, and the best of three rides wins the round."

"Why do they go slowly at first?" Bess asked. "That seems dumb. Why not sprint right from the start?"

"It's all tactics," Jon said. "Watch."

At that moment an official standing on the home straight blew his whistle. Two girls—one wearing the gray jersey of East Germany and the other the maple leaf jersey of Canada—began their ride.

A short while later, their ride over, George's first ride was announced. Her opponent was Francesca Orsini, from Italy. As Jon stood with George at the starting line, Nancy noticed something odd. "Why isn't George riding her new bike?"

"Because disk-wheel bikes don't accelerate fast enough for match sprints," Ned explained. "At least, that's what Jon said."

The ride began. George led the first lap, then slowed down dramatically in the second, glancing over her shoulder every few seconds at Francesca.

"Come on, George!" Bess shouted. She turned to Nancy. "If she goes any slower, she's going to fall over!"

Nancy nodded. George was definitely creeping around the track. It looked as though she would have to pick up the pace soon.

But George didn't. Impossibly, she went slower and slower—and slower still. Finally, to the astonishment of the spectators, both girls came to a dead halt!

"I don't believe it! How are they doing that?" Bess exclaimed.

"Yeah, those bikes don't have any brakes," Ned said, echoing her amazement.

Nancy was puzzled, too. Then, looking closely, she saw that both riders were rocking their pedals back and forth, keeping themselves upright with minuscule movements of their wheels. It was a battle of nerves. George wanted Francesca to take the lead, and Francesca wanted George to keep it.

Finally, Francesca gave up. As she started forward, the crowd cheered. Nancy smiled. Leave it to George to psych out her opponent!

But George hadn't won yet. They still had one lap to go. Nancy held her breath as the bell rang. Gradually the two picked up speed, riding high on the first turn's incline. Could George pull it off? Could she—

Suddenly George jumped. Swinging past Francesca, she shot down the incline and zoomed down the back straight.

"Go, George!" Nancy screamed.

The crowd was on its feet. George pulled two bike lengths ahead, then three. Francesca pedaled hard, but George pedaled harder. Lowering her head to the handlebars, she sped into the final turn. At the finish line she was two seconds ahead.

Half an hour later George won her second ride against Francesca, earning a place in the quarter-finals. After riding a victory lap, her arms held high in a V, she returned to the infield.

"Where's Jon?" Nancy asked as George packed up her gear.

"I'm not sure."

"Maybe he left already," Bess said.

"No. He wouldn't leave without checking with me first," George said.

"Besides," Ned added, "he promised to give me a ride home."

"Is something wrong with your car?" Bess asked.

"No, it just seemed silly to keep driving two cars here all the time since he's staying at my house. I guess he'll turn up."

"I guess so," George said, joining them. "Right now, all I want is a long, hot shower. Help me load my car, will you?"

Leaving Ned behind to wait for Jon, Nancy and Bess started toward the exit tunnel with George. As they went inside, Nancy took George's bike and hoisted it to her shoulder.

She was walking slightly behind the others, so

at first she couldn't see why George had stopped short as they approached the tunnel's exit. "What's going on?" she asked.

Then she saw for herself. Jon was standing at the end of the tunnel. A pretty blond girl had her arms around him—and they were kissing!

Chapter Four

NANCY COULDN'T BELIEVE her eyes. Was this for real? Was Jon actually two-timing George? She glanced at her friend. George was pale. Bess had her hand on her shoulder, but it was more to hold George up than to hold her back. She looked as if she were about to faint.

In front of them, the cozy scene suddenly fell apart. Angrily, Jon pushed the girl away from him. "Stop that!" he growled.

"But, Jon!" the girl whined.

"Don't touch me! Can't you get it through your head? It's over."

"No, it isn't! I still love you. And you'd still love me if you hadn't lost your memory!"

Nancy relaxed. Jon wasn't cheating on George, that was obvious. The girl had kissed *him,* not the other way around. But who was she? And what was she talking about?

They didn't have to wait long for the answers. Seconds later the girl spotted them.

"Oh, it's you," she said, glaring at George. "Nice timing. I shouldn't be surprised, though. You're real good at breaking people up, aren't you?"

George's mouth dropped open. "Me?"

"Yes, you. Jon and I are in love, or at least we were until *you* came along!"

"Jon, what's this all about?" George asked.

Jon stepped forward, fidgeting with the zipper on his windbreaker. "I'm sorry you had to find out this way, George, but it is partly true. This is Debbi Howe. She and I used to go together."

"Go together? Jon, we were practically engaged!" Debbi wailed.

"Used to?" George repeated.

"That's right. We were both on the U.S. team for the last Winter Olympics. Debbi was a speed skater, not a skier."

"We were very happy together, too," Debbi added. "They did a TV story about us and everything. Then one day someone sabotaged the bindings on Jon's skis. He took a terrible fall and banged his head. After that Jon lost his memory, and he disappeared. I thought I'd never see him again—until today."

The situation was becoming clearer to Nancy. She had known that Jon had indeed lost his memory after an accident. But most of it had come back quickly. Even the part that hadn't eventually did return with George's help. So where did Debbi fit into the picture?

George was obviously wondering the same thing. "Jon?" she asked, pulling him aside so Nancy could barely hear.

Jon swallowed hard. "I guess I should have told you about this before."

"Just tell me about it now. Are you still in love with Debbi?"

"Of course not. She was just a passing thing. It's just that—well, I was surprised to see her here. I didn't want to say anything to you until I'd had a chance to straighten things out with her."

"I see."

George didn't sound convinced. Nancy wasn't, either. There was too much hesitation in Jon's voice—too much feeling in his eyes when he looked at Debbi.

George bit her knuckle. "I don't know what to do," George said, moving closer to Nancy. Debbi could now hear her.

"Well, I have a suggestion," Debbi said hotly. "Why don't you get lost? And keep your hands off my boyfriend from now on!"

"I'm not your boyfriend anymore," Jon said. "Please stop saying that."

"I'll say it as often as I like because it's true. We belong together. You can deny it as much as you want, but I'm not going to give up. And as for the bicyclist here—"

George whitened.

"Let me tell you something," Debbi said in a threatening tone as she stepped close. "If you think you're going to keep him, just forget it. He's mine, and he always will be. I'm going to get him back—no matter what it takes."

Including murder? Nancy wondered. She didn't want to think that, but Debbi seemed so determined to steal Jon from George that anything was possible.

With a final hostile grimace at George, Debbi whirled around and stormed out to the parking lot. A second later her station wagon shot toward the exit, dust rising in a cloud. Nancy noticed a wire cage in the wagon's rear compartment and black lettering on its sides, but it was too far away for her to make out the words.

She turned to Jon. "Is that a police car?" Nancy asked. "She sure drives it like one."

"No, the cage is because her family raises purebred German shepherds," he said.

Silence fell as the car disappeared from view. No one wanted to speak. Finally, though, Jon turned to George. "Remember I said that I took off after I lost my memory?"

George nodded.

"Well, later, when I got it back, I wrote her and

said that I didn't want to see her again. I don't know how she found out I was here, but she did, and she's come to try to get me to go back with her. She's even taken a room at the Imperial Motel."

"Looks like she didn't get the message."

A minute later George and Jon said good night. Jon went back inside the velodrome to get Ned while George, Bess, and Nancy continued walking toward the now-floodlit parking lot.

"You sure let him off easy," Bess remarked acidly as she yanked open the door of George's station wagon.

"What?" George asked.

"You were too nice. If it had been me, I'd have laughed in his face. I mean, can you believe all that baloney about it being over between them?"

"It's not baloney. Well, I mean—I—"

George hesitated. She was obviously torn. She wanted to accept Jon's explanation but still had her doubts.

"Come on, Bess, give Jon a break," Nancy said as she loaded the bike into the rear.

"Why? So he can walk all over her? No way. I don't want George to get hurt."

"Neither do I. But we don't know for sure that he's lying."

"We don't know that he isn't, either."

"Just stop it, both of you!" George said, exploding suddenly. "This is between Jon and me. We'll work it out on our own, okay?"

Nancy dropped the subject. But later, as she drove away, she still felt bad for George. Worse, she knew that Debbi Howe was not the kind of girl to let the issue drop as easily as Nancy and Bess had.

The next morning Nancy sat in the Drew kitchen picking at her breakfast. Hannah Gruen, the Drews' housekeeper, had made strawberry pancakes—usually one of Nancy's favorites—but Nancy wasn't hungry that day.

Across the table Carson Drew looked over the top of his morning newspaper and studied his daughter.

"What's wrong? What happened to put that gloomy look on your face?"

Nancy smiled in spite of herself. No one knew her as well as her father did—not even Ned or Hannah.

"Okay, I give. You always drag it out of me in the end, anyway. I'm working on a new case."

"Oh? What is it this time?"

"Something very serious. Someone may be trying to kill George."

Quickly she filled her father in. As she talked, her father thoughtfully spread butter on his pancakes.

"Hmm. That's a tough one," he said when

she'd finished. "I'm not sure what to tell you, but I do have one piece of advice."

"What's that?"

He set down his knife. "Make George drop out of the Classic."

"What?"

"I mean it. Don't take chances. Those two incidents might add up to nothing, but what if someone *is* trying to kill her? The more chances the killer has, the more likely it is that he or she will be successful."

"George will never quit, Dad. The Classic is too important to her."

"More important than staying alive?"

"Well, when you put it that way, it's hard to argue. But you don't know how determined she is. I've never seen George train so hard."

"You'd better give my suggestion a shot. If you don't, you may never get a chance to reason with her again."

"But, Dad—"

The telephone rang, cutting Nancy off. Leaning backward in his chair, her father stretched toward it and lifted the receiver.

"Hello? Oh, good morning, Steven." He paused, sipping his coffee. "What? Are you serious?" He paused again. "That's shocking. Have you called the police? Good. Yes—yes, I'll be right over."

He hung up. "That was Steven Lloyd. His office was broken into last night."

"Was anything stolen?" Nancy asked.

"Yes, a new software program he was working on. He'd like me to go over there. Would you like to come along?"

Nancy smiled. She loved it when her father asked for her help. "Let's go. I'll follow you in my car."

Lloyd Software Systems, Inc., was located in a new industrial park in Summitville, not far from the velodrome and not far from River Heights. Turning into the parking lot behind her father, Nancy surveyed the beautifully landscaped lawn with interest.

There were no signs of a break-in around the low, dark-windowed building. Inside, however, was a shambles. Several police officers were milling around, while Steven Lloyd himself paced back and forth. His office door had been smashed, and papers were strewn everywhere.

"I'm telling you, Carson, I don't know what I'm going to do," he groaned. "That program was crucial. It was going to be the centerpiece of a whole new product line."

"Do you think one of your competitors stole the program?" Carson Drew asked.

"No, this guy was in business for himself," Steven replied.

"A free-lancer? How can you be sure? What about one of your employees?"

Steven shook his head. "I doubt it. An insider

wouldn't need to smash down the door. Besides, there's the note."

"What note?" Nancy asked quickly.

"Oh, didn't I mention it?" Leading them into his office, he picked up a floppy disk. "Until yesterday, my new program was on this. Take a look at what's on it now."

He slipped the disk into the A drive of the personal computer next to his desk. A moment later a message appeared.

GREETINGS, MR. LLOYD. YOUR SOFTWARE PROGRAM #5240-A HAS BEEN STOLEN. PAY ME $1,000,000 OR IT WILL BE SOLD TO ANOTHER COMPANY. INSTRUCTIONS WILL FOLLOW. HAVE A NICE DAY.

"A million dollars!" Nancy gasped. "But wait, I still don't get it. How does that prove the program was stolen by a free-lancer?"

"An insider wouldn't ask for money. He or she would take the program to a competing company and ask for a job. And he or she would get it. And the competitor would just keep the program and market it themselves."

Nancy's father nodded. "It's a lot less risky that way. I agree with Steven—this has all the characteristics of a professional working alone."

Nancy had to go along with them. There was still one point that was bothering her, however.

She turned to Steven. "Was the disk protected by a password?"

Steven nodded. "Yes, and I was the only one who knew it. That's the one thing I don't understand. How did the thief guess it?"

Nancy didn't understand, either. Even with the help of a code-breaking program, a password could take months to crack.

But the rest of the evidence was pretty straightforward. The side door to the building had been jimmied, and the security system inside had been turned off with a device that could only be used from outside. No clues there. Just more indications of a well-planned job.

By then Steven's employees had begun to drift in to work. The police questioned them one at a time, but the interrogations led nowhere. No one had worked late the night before, and no one had noticed a stranger hanging around the building the previous few days.

Finally Nancy left. She felt disappointed. When her father had asked her to come along, she had hoped she would be able to help. But there was little she could do. This was a job for the police. They had the manpower and the data network needed to solve a case of this type.

But something else was bothering her—something she had overheard Steven telling her father as she left. "I'm worried, Carson," he had said. "If I don't get that program back, it could mean the end of Lloyd Software Systems."

Was that really true? Nancy wondered. If it was, George would lose her sponsor—and with him a very promising career in cycling!

Chapter Five

THE VELODROME WAS only two minutes from Lloyd Software Systems. As she drove, Nancy's thoughts returned to what her father had said at breakfast: *"Make George drop out of the Classic."* It was good advice, but would George even listen?

At the velodrome parking lot she swung into the first available space she found. All around her people were unloading bikes and gear and talking. Locking her door, she hurried toward the stadium to find George.

Ten yards from the entrance tunnel, Nancy was stopped by Peter Cooper. Behind him, she noticed that workmen were putting up a new tent to replace the burned one. Another crew was erecting a chain-link fence in a circle around it.

"'Morning, Nancy. What do you think of our new security measure?"

"I'm glad to see it," she replied. "You're going to station a guard here to check passes, aren't you?"

"Yes. And we're going to have dogs patrolling the area, too. That should prevent any more incidents like the one we had yesterday."

"I hope so." Privately, Nancy doubted it. The tent might not burn again, but George could well be the object of a new attack.

Peter smiled. "How is George doing? Has she recovered from her close call?" he asked, pushing a hand through his rust-colored hair.

"I think so," Nancy said. "It sure didn't seem to affect her performance in the match sprint last night."

"Yes, I saw the results this morning. I'm very impressed."

"Peter," Nancy said, suddenly changing the subject, "can you tell me anything about the break-in at Lloyd Software Systems last night? I mean, something that Steven might not have wanted to tell the police?"

Peter's face clouded. "You know about that?"

"Yes, I was just over there with my father. Does Steven have any enemies—you know, a rival who might want to put him out of business?"

Peter looked uncomfortable. "Well, I don't know that I should—"

"Don't worry, you can tell me about it," she said, assuring him. "My father's working on the legal end of it."

"Well, there's really not much to tell," Peter said, relaxing. "Sure, we've got rivals, but I don't know who'd stoop to something like this."

"What about personal enemies?"

"Steven? You've got to be kidding! He's one of the best-liked, most widely admired guys in the whole software business."

"I can believe it," she said, and she meant it, too. Steven Lloyd was, in her judgment, a very decent man.

"I can tell you one thing, though." Peter's voice lowered a notch. "If that program falls into the hands of another software company, Lloyd Software Systems is sunk."

"Is the program really that big a deal?"

"You bet it is. It's going to revolutionize office computer systems. Believe me, whoever markets it first is going to be king of the mountain for at least a decade."

Nancy felt more frustrated than ever. Obviously the theft of the program was more serious than Steven had hinted.

After another minute of polite chat, Nancy turned to go.

"Oh, Nancy, will you do me a favor?" Peter asked, calling her back.

"Sure."

"When you see George, tell her that I've set up an interview with the *River Heights Morning Record.* The reporter will be here around three."

"Okay, I'll tell her."

"Thanks."

Finding George didn't turn out to be easy. Nancy looked all over the velodrome but couldn't spot her friend anywhere.

Finally, she found George sitting inconspicuously in the stands. She was talking to Tatyana Ivanova.

Tatyana was giggling. "Oh, yes, boys in Soviet Union are same. Think they know everything. Sometimes it is so funny!"

Her dark eyes were dancing, and the corners of her mouth were curled up in a smile. She looked much more relaxed than she had by the pool the day before, Nancy noticed. George was having a positive effect on her.

"Hi, Nan!" George said, looking up. "Come sit with us. Tatyana, this is my friend Nancy Drew."

"Happy to meet you," Tatyana said, offering her hand.

Nancy shook it. "I'm pleased to meet you, too. I hope you're enjoying our country."

"Oh, yes, it is very interesting."

They talked for a few minutes. Tatyana, Nancy learned, came from Leningrad. She had a sister, liked rock music, and had never heard of pizza. Just as she began to describe her impressions of America, however, a sharp voice interrupted their conversation.

"Tatyana!"

All three heads turned at once. It was the woman from the pool, the short one who had scolded Tatyana for talking with George. She was standing at the end of the aisle, looking furious.

Tatyana froze.

"You must warm up for your next ride right away," the woman said.

"But her next ride isn't for two hours," George said.

The Soviet coach ignored her remark. Hands on her hips, she stood where she was until Tatyana rose and left. When the girl was gone, she turned to George angrily.

"Miss Fayne, in the future please do not distract Tatyana from her cycling. She is very busy. She has many events in which to ride. If you persist in your attempts to ruin her concentration, the consequences will be serious."

"What!" George was aghast. "I'm not trying to ruin her concentration. I'm just trying to be her friend!"

"Call it what you like," the woman said.

"It's the truth! I'd never do that to Tatyana!"

"On the contrary, you have just demonstrated that you would."

Nancy could see that George was getting

angry, but she knew that arguing would be useless. The woman was determined to keep the two girls apart.

"George, let it go," Nancy advised in a whisper.

"No way," George said, turning toward Nancy. "She's accusing me of cheating."

"I know, but she doesn't really mean it. It's just an excuse."

"That makes it worse!"

George turned back toward the end of the aisle, but she was too late to continue the argument. The woman was gone.

"Well, how do you like that!" she remarked. "She didn't even give me a chance to defend myself."

Nancy sighed. "It wouldn't have done any good."

"I don't agree. I might have convinced her that I'm not trying to hurt Tatyana."

"I doubt that," Nancy said. "The only thing that will convince her of that is if you leave Tatyana alone."

A look of annoyance crossed George's face, then quickly disappeared. She said nothing further about the matter, but Nancy knew that it was still bothering her.

Nancy couldn't really blame her. What the KGB was doing was unfair. Still, she hoped that George would play it safe and stay away from the

Soviet girl, especially in light of the coach's warning: "If you persist in your attempts . . . the consequences will be serious."

That afternoon George won her quarter-final ride in the Women's 3,000-Meter Individual Pursuit. At the finish, she was four full seconds ahead of her opponent, Ute Alber of West Germany.

After the race George pedaled into the infield and climbed off her bike. She and Jon were barely speaking. Had they been fighting because of Debbi? Nancy wondered.

She didn't get a chance to find out. As George changed from her cycling shoes into sneakers, Peter Cooper walked up. With him was the reporter from the *River Heights Morning Record,* Marjorie Masters. Nancy had already passed along Peter's message, so George was expecting the interview.

"Hi," she said, shaking Ms. Masters's hand. "Just give me a minute to stretch out, okay? I don't want to get stiff."

George and the reporter ended up talking for twenty minutes. When they were done, Ms. Masters held up her camera case. "How about some pictures?" she asked.

"Fine," George replied.

"I noticed a good backdrop on my way into the stadium. Can we take some shots out there?"

George glanced apprehensively at her new bike. "Uh, that's a problem. You see, my bike is valuable, and I don't want to leave it untended. Normally I'd give it to Jon to watch, but he went off to get some lunch."

Nancy was about to offer to watch the bike herself when Peter Cooper suddenly spoke up. "Don't worry. I'll stay here and guard it for you."

"Thanks, Peter, but that's not necessary," George told him. "I'm sure you have more important things to do."

"It's no problem, really. Go and have your picture taken," he insisted, reaching eagerly for the bike.

"Wait a minute," Ms. Masters said. "I have an idea. Why don't you bring the bike along, George? We'll include it in the shots."

"Good idea!" George agreed.

The group walked outside. There, at a grassy area at one end of the stadium, George began to pose. Peter Cooper excused himself. He had other business to look after, he said.

"That's great, George. Okay, now turn away from the sun a little more," the reporter directed.

"How's this?" George asked, swiveling with her bike.

"Fine, fine—now smile!"

Ms. Masters resumed shooting. As she did, Nancy stood back and absently studied the grass.

Just then, a shadow appeared next to hers. She looked up. It was Ned.

"Hi. What's up?" he asked. "You've got a frown on your face."

Nancy smiled. "Nothing's up. I was just thinking."

"About what happened to George yesterday?"

"Yes, that and what happened to Steven Lloyd this morning."

Quickly she filled him in on the break-in at Lloyd Software Systems.

Ned whistled when she was finished. "Wow, it looks bad for Steven. And for George, too. She'll be devastated if she loses her sponsor."

"Not half as devastated as she'll be if she gets killed," Nancy remarked.

Ned cocked his head. "Does that mean you think the note, the burning tent, and the radio in the pool are all connected?"

"I don't know what to think," Nancy admitted. "They might be, but then again it all might be a coincidence—"

She stopped. A sixth sense was warning her that something was urgently wrong. But what was it?

Everything in sight looked normal. George and Ms. Masters were shooting photos. Behind them was the backdrop the reporter had chosen—a row of pine trees. Behind the pine trees rose a row of towering aluminum flagpoles, from which were flown the flags from the participating nations. Behind the flagpoles were the spectator stands.

The flagpoles. That was it! One of them, the one directly behind George, was out of line. It was leaning. No, it was falling—toward George!

Chapter Six

"GEORGE! LOOK OUT!" Nancy shouted.

George did not move. The flagpole was behind her, and she couldn't see it falling. "What?" she asked.

It was too late to explain. It was also too late to get to George. Nancy screamed.

Ned had already broken into a run. His long basketball player's legs churned at blinding speed. In a second he had tackled George, and the two of them were in a heap on the grass five feet away. George's bike was also clear of the pole.

The pole crashed to the ground, narrowly missing Ms. Masters. The reporter, who had been looking through her camera lens until that moment, looked up and fainted.

"Oh no," Nancy said. She didn't know what to do first. Quickly, she rushed over to the reporter. She was out cold.

"Ned, are you and George okay?" she shouted.

"Uh, fine—I think," Ned answered.

"Take care of this lady, will you? I've got to check something out!"

Rising to her feet, Nancy sprinted across the grass. When it fell, the flagpole had knocked over the pine tree directly in front of it. Nancy leaped through the gap in the line of shrubbery and looked around.

There was no one in sight. Naturally, she told herself. Why should the culprit hang around?

Conducting a search was pointless, she knew. Right then the culprit was probably busy melting into the crowd. Instead, she bent down to examine the base of the fallen flagpole.

It was just as she had expected. Normally, the base was bolted to a concrete footing with four large steel nuts, but now the nuts were off. A wrench lay nearby.

Stepping back through the gap, Nancy went over to Ned and George. They were with Ms. Masters, who was sitting up, her head tucked between her knees. "Is she okay?" Nancy asked.

"She'll be all right," Ned told her. "What did you find back there?"

"It *was* deliberate. Someone unbolted the

base, shoved the pole, then ran, using that line of pine trees as a screen."

"Huh. I guess that means—"

"Yes," Nancy finished for him. "There's no doubt about it anymore. Someone is definitely trying to kill George!"

Two hours later George won her semifinal ride in the Women's 3000-Meter Individual Pursuit. Afterward, as Nancy helped load George's gear into the station wagon, she mentally reviewed everything that had happened that afternoon.

Unfortunately, no new clues had developed from the flagpole incident. The spectators in the stands high above the scene had not noticed anything suspicious, according to the police. Neither had anyone who was outside the stadium.

Nancy had hoped the reporter's film might yield a clue, but that too had been a dead end. When Nancy phoned Ms. Masters later, the reporter told her that the newly developed pictures showed nothing but George, her bike, and the solid row of pine trees in the background.

It was mildly frustrating. Still, now she knew that the warning note and the incidents at the tent, the pool, and the flagpole were linked. Nancy became absolutely determined to find the culprit.

But where to begin with no clues? Nancy felt frustrated and totally helpless.

When George's car was loaded, Nancy, Ned, George, and Jon drove to Big Top Burgers in River Heights for dinner. Bess met them there. She had been to the dentist that afternoon and had not been at the velodrome.

"How'd it go today?" she asked her cousin after they had ordered and begun to eat.

"Great," George said, sliding into the booth. "Thanks to the bike, I won the semi in pursuit. And guess who I'm up against in the final?"

"Who?"

"Monique Vandervoort, the World Junior Champion!" George said proudly.

"Wow, that's great! Sounds like it was a pretty exciting day," Bess remarked.

"Yeah, it was exciting, all right," Jon said sourly.

An uncomfortable silence fell. Everyone was thinking about the flagpole incident and what it meant, Nancy knew.

"Is someone going to tell me what's going on?" Bess asked after a minute.

"Nothing's going on," George mumbled, poking at her food.

"Oh yeah? Then why the long faces?" Bess demanded.

Briefly, Nancy filled her in. When Nancy was finished, Bess folded her napkin and slapped it down on the tabletop.

"I don't believe you! How can you take this so

calmly, George? Someone is trying to kill you, don't you understand that?"

George nodded. "Sure, but what do you expect me to do about it?"

"Drop out of the Classic. Now—tonight."

For a moment no one spoke. Bess had said what was on everyone's mind but what everyone had been afraid to suggest.

"Forget it," George said at last. "I'm not dropping out."

"What?" Bess cried, her voice ringing with disbelief.

"I said, I'm staying in the competition. I've been training for it for months. Jon came all the way to River Heights just to coach me. I'd be crazy to quit."

"You're crazy to keep going," Bess argued. "I'm not saying that you should give up cycling forever. All I'm saying is that you should stop for this week."

"No way."

"George, listen to me—"

"No, you listen to me!" she interrupted. "If there's one thing I'm not, it's a quitter. I'm not going to act like a coward just because somebody's trying to scare me a little."

The cousins glared at each other. It was an impasse. Bess wasn't going to back down, and neither was George.

"Ooh!" Bess smacked the table in fury. She

turned to Jon. "Would you please talk some sense into her?"

Everyone looked at Jon.

"Uh, I don't know what to say. I mean, I'd hate to see George quit, but I don't see any other choice."

"Jon!" George cried.

"Well, I don't!"

"I can't believe this! I can't believe you're siding with Bess!"

"George, all the training in the world is useless if you're dead," Jon reasoned.

"But I'm alive! I'm not dead! What do you want me to do, sit at home all day by myself?" she asked, beginning to cry.

"Come on. Why would I want that?" Jon asked.

"Why? Why else?" George said, choking back a sob. "So you can be with Debbi!"

Quickly George pushed out of the booth and stood up. Her sleeve brushed a water glass, and it fell to the floor. Everyone in the restaurant turned to look.

Silence descended, and in the sudden quiet George's sobs echoed loudly. But only for a moment. A second later she was gone.

"Great. Now you've done it," Ned said, snapping at Bess as the exit door swung closed.

"Don't blame me," Bess fired back. "I'm not the one who's two-timing!"

At that, Jon quietly left the booth and went

after George. As she watched him go, Nancy frowned. Would he be able to patch things up between them?

Watching through the window, she saw Jon catch up with George in the parking lot. They began to talk. To Nancy's relief, she could see George slowly begin to relax. After a few minutes, she even smiled and threw her arms around him.

Nancy relaxed, too. At least she didn't have to worry about George and Jon anymore, she thought. Her only problem now was getting the boxing gloves off Ned and Bess. They were still arguing.

Suddenly Ned broke off in the middle of what he was saying. He grabbed Nancy's arm. "Look outside!" he said.

Nancy again turned her gaze toward the window. A smiling Jon was walking back toward the restaurant, and George was walking toward her car.

"Yes, I already—"

"Look!"

Then she saw it. A pair of headlights snapped from low to high. Then suddenly she heard squealing tires. A car accelerated and was heading straight for George!

Chapter Seven

WHAT HAPPENED NEXT was difficult to follow. The car gunning for George was also pointed right at the window. In the dusky twilight the glare from its headlights made it difficult for Nancy to see.

For a moment George was silhouetted alone in the light. Then, as the car zoomed closer, a second silhouette flew into the picture and shoved George out of the way—Jon!

Nancy's heart skipped a beat. "Come on, let's go!" she said to Ned and Bess.

As they scrambled from their seats, the car swerved to the right, missing Jon by inches. The next second it shot past the restaurant window and sped out of view. Nancy heard its tires shriek as it turned into the road.

Outside, Nancy sprinted to the end of the entrance drive, hoping to get a better look at the car.

But all she spotted were the red taillights as they disappeared around a distant corner. The license plate was also a blur.

Disappointed, she walked back to check on Jon and George. Both of them would be bruised, but otherwise they were okay. A small crowd was gathering around them.

"That was a close call," Jon said, wiping the dirt from his hands.

George put her arms around him. "Too close! If anything had happened to you—"

"Luckily, nothing did," Ned commented. "What I want to know is, who was driving that thing? Did anyone get a look?"

Jon shook his head. "Not me."

George shook her head, too. "I was looking at Jon."

Nancy, Ned, and Bess hadn't seen who it was, either. Nor had anyone else in the restaurant. Nancy questioned people in the crowd, but all of them had either been looking somewhere else or, like her, had been blinded by the glare of the car's headlights in the window.

"Whoever planned that attack was either very lucky or very smart," Nancy remarked.

"Are you sure it was planned?" Jon asked.

"Well, it wasn't an accident!"

Suddenly George cried, "Wait a minute —check out my car!"

Everyone turned. The station wagon's rear gate was wide open. Together, Nancy, Ned, George, Jon, and Bess ran across the lot.

George got there first. "Oh, thank goodness! My bike is still there!"

"Yeah, but the car's in pretty bad shape," Ned said with a frown.

It certainly was. The rear window had been smashed, and there were scratches in the paint around the rear door lock.

"Looks like someone was trying to steal the bike," Jon said.

"Maybe," Nancy replied.

"Only maybe?" Bess asked.

"It's equally possible that whoever it was saw George leave the restaurant and smashed the window to make it *look* like a theft attempt."

"You know, I did hear glass breaking as I came out," George said.

"I don't get it," Jon put in. "If the crook wasn't trying to steal the bike, then what *was* he trying to do?"

"Sabotage it," Nancy said grimly.

Ned nodded. "That would explain the scratches around the lock. At first the killer tried to break in, but then, when he saw George, he changed his plan—to a hit-and-run."

Bess shivered.

"So who was it?" George asked after a minute had passed.

"I'm not sure," Nancy said tightly. "But there's one way we might be able to find out. Ned, can you come with me? I may need your help."

Ten minutes later Nancy pulled her Mustang into the parking lot of the Imperial Motel. Every single space was occupied.

"Good. This should be easy," she said.

"What are you going to do?" Ned asked her.

Nancy parked near the front office. "Come on. I'll show you."

Climbing out, she walked over to the first row of parked cars. One by one, she placed her hand on the hoods.

Ned joined her. "I get it. You're feeling for warm engines."

"Uh-huh. If someone wanted to tamper with George's bike, it would probably be someone who's staying here. I want to see if any of these cars have been driven recently."

Down the row she went, pausing at each hood. The parking spaces were numbered, and Nancy noticed that each number corresponded to the room closest to it.

"This one's warm," Ned said. His hand was on the hood of a subcompact.

Nancy felt it. "Yes, but not warm enough. That car was really going fast when it hit the road. That engine was hot!"

Finally, Nancy jerked her hand back sharply from a sizzling hood. Stepping back, she surveyed the car. It was a station wagon. Black lettering decorated its doors, and a dog cage filled the rear compartment. It was Debbi Howe's car!

"Room one fifty-five," Ned said.

The door was right in front of them. The windows were dark. Marching up to the door, Nancy rapped loudly. A muffled voice answered from inside, and a minute later the door swung open.

Debbi was wearing a blue cotton nightgown, and she looked at Nancy and Ned sleepily. But her nightgown wasn't wrinkled, and Nancy noticed her hair wasn't tousled, either.

"What do you two want?" Debbi asked.

"We want to talk to you."

"Forget it. I'm going back to sleep."

"Really?" Nancy couldn't keep the impatience from her voice. "If you were asleep, just who was driving your car?"

Debbi scowled at her. "What is this, some kind of joke?"

"No," Nancy said. "The hood of your car is red hot. It's been driven recently."

"So? What if it was?"

Nancy narrowed her eyes. "Someone tried to run George Fayne down tonight."

"Look, smarty," Debbi hissed. "I don't know what you're getting at, but whatever it is, I don't like it. Why don't you just get lost?"

"Not until I get some answers." The door was closing, but Nancy stopped it with her foot. "Were you or weren't you in the parking lot of Big Top Burgers tonight?"

"I wasn't."

Nancy pressed her point. "Then how did your car engine get so hot?"

"Look, if you must know, I drove over to Riley City to see some friends," Debbi confessed. "I just got back."

That would explain where her car had been, but was she telling the truth? "You can prove you were there?" Nancy asked.

"Yes. But why should I?"

"Because—" Nancy stopped, not sure what to say next.

"Because you think I was somewhere else, right? Well, let me tell you something. I don't care what you think. You're not the police. If you were, I'd prove to you that I was in Riley City. But you're not, so leave me alone!"

With that, she started to shut the door again, but once more Nancy stopped her.

"Look, Debbi," she said angrily, "someone tried to run George down tonight. At the very least, I think you know who it was."

"So?"

"So, I suggest you confess. If you're honest now, things will be easier later. But if you lie—"

"Then what?"

"I mean it, Debbi."

"Good for you," she said. "Now, get this—I didn't try to run down your friend. But maybe she'd better watch out from now on," Debbi added. "If the opportunity presents itself, I just might try to hurt her."

This time when Debbi slammed her door, Nancy didn't stop her.

When Nancy arrived home later, she was furious with herself. Debbi had outbluffed her. She was almost sure that Jon's ex-girlfriend had tried to hit George, but she couldn't prove a thing.

Worse, it was her own fault. She'd lost her temper and tipped Debbi off. Right then, Debbi was probably putting together a rock-solid alibi. Even if Nancy went to the police, it wouldn't do any good. When they questioned Debbi, the first thing she would do was prove that she'd been visiting friends in Riley City that night.

Nancy climbed out of her car and slammed the door. On her way into the house, she noticed that Steven Lloyd's car was also parked in the driveway.

The two men were in her father's study discussing the break-in at Steven's office. It had only happened that morning, but to Nancy it seemed as if it were a week ago.

"Have the police got any leads?" she asked, joining them.

"Not really," Steven said.

Nancy frowned. "The guy hasn't called to tell you where to drop the money?"

"No," he replied, shaking his head. "What's he waiting for?"

Behind his desk, Carson Drew leaned back. "Count your blessings, Steven. Raising a million in cash isn't easy on such short notice."

"No. And I really appreciate all your help."

Both men glanced at the blue nylon gym bag that was sitting on the desk. With a jolt, Nancy realized that it must contain the money—one million dollars.

She dropped into a leather club chair. One million dollars. That must be some program, she thought. Too bad the police didn't have any leads yet.

Just then the telephone rang. Nancy's father scooped up the receiver and held it to his ear. Seconds later he sat up straighter, and his eyes grew wide.

He handed the phone to Steven. "It's our man," he whispered. "You'll have to listen hard. His voice is being distorted by some sort of electronic device."

Steven took the receiver. "Hello? Yes . . . yes . . ."

The conversation was short. Nancy's heart was pounding with excitement. Leaning forward, she put her elbows on her knees.

"Well, we've got instructions," Steven said as he hung up. "He definitely wants a million."

"Where and when?" Carson Drew asked.

Steven's face clouded. "That's the strange part—he didn't say."

"What!"

"He said he'd call back with further instructions."

"When?"

"He didn't say."

"Hmm." Nancy's father leaned back and pressed his fingertips together, looking puzzled. "But what's most strange is how he knew to call you here."

"Good question," Steven replied. "I didn't tell anyone I was coming over, not even my secretary."

"You're sure?"

"Positive. I wrote it in my date book, but . . ."

For a moment no one spoke. Why didn't the extortionist want the money right away? It didn't make sense. Nancy turned the point over and over in her mind, but no explanation presented itself.

Finally, Steven cleared his throat. "Carson . . ." he began, sounding uncomfortable.

"Yes?"

"The extortionist also mentioned the courier.

When the time comes, he doesn't want me to carry the money myself."

"Oh? Who does he want?" Nancy's father asked.

Steven swallowed and looked down. "I don't know how to tell you this, but he—he wants Nancy!"

Chapter Eight

THERE WAS SILENCE for a few seconds. The only sound was the ticking of the brass clock on Carson Drew's desk. Finally, Nancy's father shook his head.

"Absolutely not," he said firmly. "I won't allow it."

Steven leaned back in his chair, obviously relieved. "I'm glad you said that. If anything were to happen to Nancy, I would never forgive myself."

Nancy looked at the two men. "Wait a minute. Don't I get to say anything?"

Both men turned and stared at her.

"I want to carry the money," she said. "For

one thing, the extortionist probably sees me as insurance. He knows you won't try anything funny because you don't want me to get hurt. That means—"

"Nancy—"

"No, listen! That means he might get careless and slip up. I could pick up some clues. I might even see his face!"

"You know, Carson—" Steven started to say.

"I'll be perfectly safe. You and Steven will be tailing me in a car, right, Dad? The police will be there, too."

"Now, Nancy—"

"Please, Dad?"

Her father sighed. "I can see this is a losing battle. All right, I'll let you do it. But I want you to promise me that you'll drop the money and run at the first sign of trouble."

Nancy smiled and nodded. "I'm not crazy, Dad."

"Good. Now, Steven, are you absolutely sure you want to pay the ransom?"

"I know you think I shouldn't," Steven replied. "But frankly that program is worth a lot more to my company than one million dollars."

"It's your choice." Carson Drew reached for the phone. "I'm going to call the police. Now that Nancy's involved, I want them to be ready to roll at a moment's notice."

* * *

The next afternoon Nancy paced restlessly around the infield of the velodrome. She was as concerned about George as ever—more, really. And now added to that worry were new questions about the theft of Steven's program.

Why did the extortionist want her to deliver the money? The reason she had given her father —that she was an "insurance policy"—made sense, but it didn't explain everything. Also, how had the extortionist known that her father was involved in the case? How had he known to call Steven at the Drew residence?

George, meanwhile, seemed unfazed by the attempt to kill her the day before. If anything, she seemed more energetic than ever. When she lost her quarter-final ride in the Women's Match Sprint, she shrugged it off. "I'm saving myself for the Pursuit finals tonight," she claimed.

That evening a large crowd gathered at the velodrome. Marjorie Masters's article about George had appeared in the *River Heights Morning Record* that day, and many people had come to see whether their hometown girl could defeat the reigning World Junior Champion.

But Monique Vandervoort was not going to give up her title without a struggle. As the two raced around and around the track, the Dutch girl really poured on the speed.

Anxiously, Nancy watched the scoreboard that stood at the north end of the stadium. Each time

George and Monique crossed their respective starting lines, their times were displayed. George was behind, Nancy saw, but she could still recover. Could she take the lead?

The spectators cheered. They were behind George all the way. Then, at the beginning of the fifth lap, Jon called out something to George as she flew by. After that, George took off. The next split showed that she'd gained a second. She was only one and two-tenths seconds behind!

Nancy's heart was pounding. There were three laps left to go—then two—then one. *Come on, George,* she cried silently. *Come on!*

George flashed around the final turns, but Monique was struggling, tired by her early effort. As they finished, Nancy watched the scoreboard. When the final times appeared, she let out a whoop. George had won by two-tenths of a second!

After the race, well-wishers crowded around George. Everywhere flashes exploded. George was beaming, and her smile broadened even more when Steven Lloyd and Peter Cooper came over.

"Congratulations!" Steven said, clapping her on the back.

"Thanks. I couldn't have done it without this bike."

"I'm glad it helped."

Peter cleared his throat. "Uh, speaking of the bike, I heard what happened at Big Top Burgers last night. Would you like me to keep it locked in the administrative office at night? It might be safer there."

"Thanks. But you don't have to worry. I found a great place to hide it when I'm not using it. No one will ever think to look there, believe me."

"Are you sure? Because it's no trouble to lock it up in our office if you want."

Steven put his hand on his assistant's shoulder. "Pete, I think we can trust George to look after the bike," he said.

"Don't worry. I'm not going to let anyone get near that bike," George agreed with a smile.

Peter opened his mouth to say something more, but he got cut off. At just that moment a reporter from a cycling magazine fired a question at George. At the same time, Steven pulled Nancy aside for a whispered conference.

"Still no word from the extortionist," he said anxiously.

"Don't worry, he'll call soon," Nancy assured him in a low voice.

"I hope so. I'm worried about my program."

"And he's worried about that million dollars. Sit tight."

"I'm trying, but it's tough," Steven said. "This whole thing has me on edge."

Nancy was on edge, too, but for another reason. George's would-be killer was still at large. She was positive she would eventually figure out who it was, but she didn't like waiting. It left George in constant danger.

She didn't want to burden Steven with all that, though. After a few minutes he said good night. He was going home to wait by his telephone, he told her.

Nancy wished him luck.

Later, after calling her father and being told that the extortionist still hadn't called yet, Nancy went to George's house. She and Bess were going to sleep over. George needed the company, Bess had told her, and Nancy agreed. Her father could reach her at the Faynes' house if anything happened. Besides, it would give the three of them a chance to talk.

As it turned out, however, the one who was anxious to talk was George's mother. "Nancy, can I have a word with you?" she asked as the girls were leaving the Faynes' kitchen.

"Sure, Mrs. Fayne," Nancy said, holding a bowl of popcorn.

"It's Georgia—" Louise Fayne broke off distractedly. "Oh, Nancy, will you try to persuade Georgia to drop out of the Classic? It's so risky! I'm afraid for her!"

"She won't listen to me, I've tried. You're her mother, though. Have you told her how you feel?"

"Yes, this morning at breakfast. She said, 'No

way!' " Mrs. Fayne laughed weakly. "After that, I gave up. You know Georgia, she can be stubborn."

"Yes, I know."

Nancy bounded up the stairs to George's room. George and Bess were sitting cross-legged on the bed, watching TV.

"Did you get more popcorn?" George asked, looking up.

"Plenty."

"Great." George dug into the bowl as Nancy set it down. "My mom asked you to get me to drop out of the Classic, didn't she?"

Nancy nodded. "How did you know?"

"I just did. She and my dad were on my case at breakfast, too."

Bess picked up the remote control and turned down the TV's sound. "George, would it really be so bad to drop out?"

"Yes," she replied firmly.

"But—"

"Let's not get into that again, okay?" George pleaded. "I don't want to fight, and besides, there's something more important that I want to talk to you guys about."

"What?" Nancy asked.

"Jon. His birthday's coming up, and I need to think of a present."

"How about a one-way ticket back to the mountains?" Bess said acidly.

"Bess!"

"I mean it. How can you trust him after you saw him kissing his old girlfriend? The guy still loves her, believe me!"

"No he doesn't! He told me so last night in the Big Top parking lot. And then he saved my life not a minute later."

"So? What does that prove?" Bess shot back.

The two argued on and on, Bess tearing Jon apart and George defending him. Nancy stayed out of it. She was just glad to hear that George and Jon were on good terms again.

An hour later Nancy and Bess crawled into their sleeping bags. George turned out the lights, but they all kept talking. When the conversation finally ended, the dial on the digital clock by George's bed read 12:15 A.M.

Almost an hour later Nancy was still awake. Details of the case—Monique at the motel window, the Soviet coach's warning, the warm hood of Debbi's car—kept running through her mind. Next to her, Bess was breathing evenly. Across the room in her bed, George was also asleep.

Rolling onto her back, Nancy folded her hands behind her head and stared at the ceiling. The house was quiet. Through a window, she heard a light breeze pass. The oak trees on the lawn rustled gently.

Suddenly Nancy tensed. She thought she'd heard a sound, but she wasn't sure.

Creak!

Yes, there it was again. This time there was no mistaking it.

Someone was sneaking up the stairs!

Chapter Nine

SILENTLY, NANCY SLITHERED from her sleeping bag. Standing up, she tiptoed to the doorway and listened.

Creak!

The intruder was almost at the top of the stairs. She had to do something.

Mentally, Nancy reviewed the layout of George's room. There was a softball bat in the corner—or was it in the closet? No good. She needed something else. The desk chair! That was it. It was right next to her sleeping bag. Tiptoeing back, she groped in the dark and found it.

She lifted the chair over her head.

Creak!

Once again Nancy tiptoed back to the door. It was very dark. She couldn't see a thing. The door was ajar, she remembered. Feeling with her foot, she found it and pushed it open. Now the way into the hall was clear.

Anxiously, she peered into the void ahead. Should she attack now? Go for it, she told herself. Whoever's out there can't see, either.

Slowly, she took a step forward. Then another. And another. Then—*whack!* The chair hit the doorjamb overhead! Angry, Nancy tried to lower the chair, but she lost her grip. The chair fell to the floor with a crash.

"What was that?" George exclaimed in a loud voice.

Footsteps hurried down the stairs. The intruder was getting away! Nancy groped for the hall light switch. She flicked it on just as the front door slammed.

"Mr. Fayne! George! Follow me!"

Furious with herself, Nancy raced down the stairs and through the front hall. If she hurried, she could still get a look at the intruder.

Yanking the door open, she dashed out onto the front lawn. She glanced around but didn't see anyone. Great! She'd let the intruder get away!

"Nancy?"

The front porch lights came on. Nancy blinked. Mr. Fayne's deep voice called out again. "Nancy, are you okay?"

"I'm fine, Mr. Fayne."

"What happened?"

She walked back across the lawn. "There was an intruder in the house, but he got away."

Just then, George, Bess, and Mrs. Fayne spilled down the stairs, shouting questions all at once. Mr. Fayne reassured them that everything was all right, but Mrs. Fayne was still frightened.

To calm her, Mr. Fayne made a thorough search of the property.

"I don't believe you, Nan," Bess said when Nancy had explained what happened. They were standing in the kitchen. "You actually tried to clobber the burglar with a chair?"

"Actually, I don't think it was a burglar," Nancy said. "I think it may have been someone who didn't know that George had a couple of friends sleeping over tonight."

"You mean—"

Mr. Fayne walked in, interrupting Bess. "Yes, that's exactly what she means. And I'm afraid she may be right. Come and look at what I found outside!"

Quickly, they followed him out to the driveway. He pointed his flashlight at the front of the garage door.

Mrs. Fayne gasped. On the door was the picture of George that had been in the newspaper. It was pinned in place with a gleaming butcher knife!

* * *

The next morning Nancy set out for the Imperial Motel. She was angry. The picture on the Faynes' garage door had been the last straw. No one had the right to terrorize innocent people and get away with it. No one!

Nancy parked in front of the bank next door to the Imperial. Her car wouldn't be noticed there. Then, pulling a straw hat over her reddish gold hair, and putting on a pair of sunglasses, she began her surveillance.

It was a hot day, and a few people were already in the pool. Walking up to the soda machine behind the front office, Nancy pretended to study the selection. From there, she eyed the people at the pool. Debbi was not among them. No problem, she thought. She knew which room was Debbi's.

Casually, Nancy walked past Debbi's room. She could hear the TV but nothing else. Just then, the phone rang and Debbi picked it up, saying, "Oh, hi, Mom."

Nancy's heart began to thump as she listened through the door. Perfect! She could hear every word.

"Sure, I remember," Debbi said in a sullen tone. "I had to go out last night—I couldn't wait for your call. . . . I'm sorry. Yes, it was very late when I got back—about two. . . . Uh-huh, I'm learning a lot about racing. It could be a good sport for me with the skating. Okay, yeah. I'll be home soon. . . . Yeah, I promise, no more late nights. . . ."

Nancy couldn't believe her luck. She had the evidence she had come for, so she hurried back to her car.

"She did what?" Ned asked.

Nancy had gone over to the velodrome. Ned, Bess, and George were gathered around her in the parking lot, their mouths hanging open.

"I said, she was out last night until two A.M.! That's not proof, of course, but it's quite a coincidence."

"So it could have been Debbi who was creeping around my house with a butcher knife last night!" George said.

"That's how it looks to me."

"I can't believe it. Who'd have thought she'd actually try to kill me?"

"I'm not surprised," Bess said, crossing her arms. "A man stealer like that would try anything, I bet."

Ned shook his head and sighed. "I'm sorry, Bess, but I can't agree. Sure, Debbi wants to get Jon back, but murdering George to do it? That's too extreme. I don't think we have enough evidence."

Nancy listened with mixed feelings. At first she'd been excited, but now she wasn't so sure. Ned was right. The evidence was very circumstantial.

Ned rubbed his chin. "Then again, I could be wrong. After all, Debbi *is* the best suspect we've got. What do you think, Nancy?"

"Well, of all the suspects in the case, Debbi looks as good as anyone," Nancy said slowly. "Every time something's happened, she's had the opportunity to do it."

"So what are we waiting for?" Bess asked.

"Better evidence. When we go to the police, I want them to be convinced that we're right."

Just then, Jon walked up. "Hi, everyone. What's going on?"

Quickly, Nancy told him. She had expected him to react badly—after all, he *had* been in love with Debbi—but she wasn't prepared for the guilty look on his face.

"I don't know how to tell you this," he said, looking down. His face was red. "I guess I have to, though—"

"Tell us what, Jon?" George asked.

"Debbi couldn't have been the one who was in your house. She was with me last night."

Chapter Ten

AFTER JON'S ADMISSION, things went a little crazy. Everyone began talking at once. While Nancy mentally assessed the damage to her theory, George kept asking Jon what he was doing with Debbi at that hour.

"It's not what you think," Jon explained, looking down at his hands. "She still wouldn't leave me alone, so last night I took her out to try to convince her once and for all that we're finished. She wouldn't believe it at first, and that's why we were out so late."

"Yeah, right," Bess said.

George was sniffling. "How could you do that without telling me?"

"I-I'm sorry, George. I didn't want to ruin your concentration."

"Why not? We said we'd share everything with each other, didn't we?"

"Yes, but—"

"You should have shared this with me. Especially this!" George was crying openly. "I can't believe this is happening," she said in a small voice. "I just can't believe it. I trusted you!"

Jon said nothing.

"Well, no more. That's it," George continued. "You can keep coaching me if you want, but otherwise our relationship is over."

"George! Come on, you don't mean that."

"Yes I do! I mean it. We're through. Don't call me anymore."

"But, George—"

Turning, she ran off. Bess shot Jon an icy glare and followed her cousin. When they were gone, Nancy, Ned, and Jon were left together. An awkward silence fell. Jon looked devastated.

Nancy felt miserable. She wanted to believe Jon's story, but at the same time she understood George's feelings. Jon should have told her the truth. What a complete and total mess!

And that didn't even take into consideration her case! *That* was also a shambles. Debbi was out as a suspect, and now all she had left were questions.

* * *

Later that day George rode in the Women's Points Race. All the contestants started together, and every fifth lap they sprinted for points. Whoever had the most points after fifty laps won the race.

A lot of strategy was involved in a points race, but Nancy didn't pay close attention. She was still mulling over the dramatic turnaround in the case.

About halfway through the race, Nancy looked up. It was a sprint lap. George and Monique Vandervoort were leading the field, sprinting side by side at forty miles an hour. All at once Monique swerved sharply. Forced off balance, George fell.

A gasp of horror rose from the stands. The spectators stood. On the track, George spun around twice. Because her feet were locked to the pedals, she couldn't move.

A second later the other riders reached George. Two of them plowed into her and toppled over. More followed.

All over the infield, coaches, trainers, and support crews began to run. Nancy took off, too. But Jon reached the scene first, and by the time Nancy arrived he had already pulled both George and her bike from the track. Quickly, he unlocked her feet from the pedals, and George stood up.

"Are you all right?" Nancy asked.

George leaned over and braced her hands on her knees. When she had caught her breath, she nodded. "Yeah, I'm fine."

"But look at your arms!" Nancy exclaimed.

George checked them. They were raw and bleeding. "Oh, that's just a little road rash," she said, smiling weakly.

Nancy was horrified, but before she could say another word, Peter Cooper ran up. "George, are you okay? Let's get you to the medic table. Here. I'll take this—"

Grabbing her bike, he began to wheel it away.

"No, leave it!" George said.

Peter stopped, a mixture of confusion and anger on his face.

"I'm going back in."

"What?" Nancy gasped. "George, you've got to be kidding!"

George shook her head. "The rules say I have three laps to rejoin the field."

"B-but the bike—!" Peter stammered. "Surely it's ruined after that pileup."

Without a word, Jon snatched it from Peter's hands. Lifting it, he spun the pedals. The rear wheel turned freely.

"It's fine. Here you go, George."

"No!" There was genuine horror in Peter's voice, but it was too late. As he spoke, George climbed back on and began to ride along the apron. One lap later she picked up speed and smoothly slipped into the field of riders.

The crowd cheered. The only person who wasn't impressed was Peter. Nancy turned to speak to him, but her comment stuck in her throat. His eyes were blazing. He looked furious. She began to wonder why, but her attention was drawn back to George.

For several laps she had been sitting in —drafting at the back of the field. Then, slowly, she began to attack, challenging Monique. In each of the remaining sprints, George won points. When the race was over, the scoreboard gave her twenty-seven to the Dutch girl's twenty-nine.

Then there was an announcement: "Ladies and gentlemen, may I have your attention please. The judges have ruled that rider number seventeen, Monique Vandervoort of Holland, has been disqualified."

George was the official winner! Smiling happily, she posed for pictures in the infield. Nancy watched, wondering how long George's smile would last. She still had her breakup with Jon to adjust to. Or would they get back together? Could she forgive him?

George also had to cope with Monique. As the photographers drifted away, the Dutch girl walked up and stared unblinkingly at her. Nancy stepped close.

"You won with a trick," Monique hissed in lightly accented English.

"What?" George asked, surprised.

"You do not deserve to win the race. You cheated."

George was shocked. "I cheated? What about you? I know that swerve wasn't accidental. You did it deliberately to make me fall!"

"That is what you say!" Monique smiled nastily.

"That's what the judges said, too."

Monique's smile changed to a hostile frown. "I warn you, George Fayne, do not try to challenge me anymore."

"Oh no? Why not?" George returned her frown.

"Because you may have another accident."

Nancy's ears perked up.

"So far you have come out okay," Monique continued. "But next time—next time, I promise, you will not be so lucky."

Chapter Eleven

THAT EVENING THE extortionist phoned Steven Lloyd. The instructions that Steven repeated to Carson Drew were simple. Within ten minutes Nancy was ready.

At precisely 9:59 P.M. Nancy—wearing jeans, tennis shoes, and a plain white shirt that would enable anyone to follow her even in the dark—stepped into the phone booth at the corner of Main and Maple. Behind her was the all-night drugstore. Half a block away, her father and Steven Lloyd waited in a car. Half the detectives in the River Heights police department were also nearby in unmarked cars, but Nancy couldn't see them.

Closing the door of the booth, Nancy dropped the heavy gym bag she was carrying onto the floor and checked her watch. The numbers were changing. It was exactly 10:00 P.M.

She waited.

And waited.

The phone did not ring. Then she suddenly noticed a slip of paper tucked into the coin return. Her heart leaped. Grabbing it, she unfolded it and read:

> You have exactly twenty minutes to reach your final destination. If you do not make it, the program will be sold. Your next instructions are in the phone booth at the corner of Main and First. Run.

Main and First—that was five blocks away! She would have to hustle. Dropping the note, she grabbed the gym bag, yanked open the door, and took off.

Five blocks later, she was breathing hard. The bag was awkward and it made running difficult. Were her father and Steven following her? Probably, but she couldn't stop to check. The first note had said that she had only twenty minutes, and she had just used up three.

Spotting the phone booth at the corner of a gas-station lot, Nancy sprinted up, pushed through the door, and stuck her finger into the coin return to retrieve the next note.

> Two blocks north. Two blocks west. Go diagonally across the field. Next note in the clown's mouth.

The clown's mouth? A field? Nancy didn't have time to stop and think. She memorized the instructions, then turned and ran.

Four blocks later, she came to the back of the high school. A vast, dark football field stretched in front of her. That explained the "field" part, anyway. She ran across the field. Glancing at the illuminated dial of her watch, she saw it was 10:09. She ran even faster.

Finally, on the other side, she stopped and looked around. There! A block away she spotted the abandoned miniature golf course, which had been closed for years. She dashed across the street and jumped the low chain-link fence. There was a carved wooden clown in the middle of the course. She stuck her hand into its red-lipped mouth. The note she found inside read:

> Two blocks north. Cross the interstate. Cross lot. Next note tucked under windshield wiper.

"This is getting ridiculous," Nancy said out loud, catching her breath.

She especially didn't want to cross the interstate. It was a major limited-access highway, and although *she* could get across it fine, for her backups it would be a wall. In order to follow her, they would have to take a long detour. They would definitely lose sight of her.

Still, there was no choice. Time was quickly running out. Shifting the gym bag to her other hand, Nancy sprinted on.

A few minutes later Nancy read the final note. She was standing in a huge, empty parking lot. Ahead of her loomed the tall, blank rear wall of a building. It was the River Heights aquarium, Oceanworld!

The note said that she should pull open the metal security door at the back of the building. There was only one, so she had no trouble finding it. She went inside.

It was 10:23. She was late.

Inside, Nancy paused to get her bearings. A hall stretched ahead of her. Jogging down it, she turned a corner and found herself in a room full of thick glass windows. Behind them, illuminated by soft green lights, were tanks of exotic fish.

"I don't believe this," she whispered.

Glancing down, she checked the note in her hand:

Door marked private. Upstairs. Leave money on catwalk.

Suddenly Nancy was nervous. She was very aware that she was alone—and vulnerable. True, the extortionist probably wouldn't hurt her—not until he got the money, anyway—but she would have felt better if she knew her father was nearby. But he was probably miles away. Should she go on?

Nancy decided to continue. She had the money, after all. If the extortionist showed up, she would simply drop it and run. He'd choose the money over chasing her.

The door marked Private was across the room. Nancy walked over and pulled it open, then tiptoed up the stairs.

At the top was another door. Pulling it open, Nancy stepped through and found herself on a narrow catwalk, just as the note had promised. What the note had not told her, however, was that the catwalk was suspended over the exhibit tanks. Below her a killer shark was swimming in circles!

Nancy shuddered. She had seen sharks before, but always from the *other* side of the glass. Being less than four feet from one was definitely not her idea of fun.

Nancy quickly dropped the gym bag onto the metal grating at her feet. Then she reached back with her hand for the doorknob.

As she was groping, she suddenly felt a hand on her back!

She screamed, but there was no one to hear. There was nothing to grab onto. She was falling, clawing wildly at the air as she fell into the tank.

Chapter Twelve

THE WATER WAS cold, and she gasped as she surfaced and blinked the drops from her eyes. The catwalk was empty. The gym bag was gone. All she saw was the back of a figure disappearing through the door, which banged shut immediately.

Then she remembered. Somewhere below her, swimming around in circles, was a shark, capable of killing her with one snap of its jaws. She had to get out of there!

Looking around frantically, she noticed that a two-foot-wide lip ran around the top of the tank. If she could get to that, she'd be okay. She could walk around it, then haul herself back up to the catwalk.

Just then, something nudged her leg and moved past her in the water. Nancy wanted desperately to scream, but she kept herself under control. Stay calm, she told herself. Just stay calm.

All at once Nancy remembered something she'd read in a book—sharks were attracted by erratic motion. If that was true, she reasoned, then maybe she could make the shark ignore her by swimming evenly through the water, with smooth, regular strokes.

It worked. Seconds later, Nancy pulled herself up onto the lip of the tank and stood. Stepping carefully, she picked her way around the tank until she reached the catwalk. Then she hauled herself up.

Two minutes later she was back outside in the parking lot. No one was there. For a moment Nancy stood absolutely still, breathing in the warm, sweet night air.

Then, as loudly as she could, she screamed.

An hour later Nancy had changed into dry clothes and was sitting in her father's study. Both her father and Steven Lloyd were there, and they were furious about what had happened.

Steven had balled his hands into fists. "If I ever get my hands on that guy—"

"You!" Nancy said, interrupting him. "Forget

it. Wait until I get *my* hands on him! He didn't even leave your program."

"I expected that," Steven said. "When I mentioned it on the phone earlier, he said he couldn't make any promises. That made me suspicious."

"Do you think he'll try to extort more money?"

"No, but I think he'll try to get the full amount that he asked for originally."

Carson Drew rose from his chair in anger. "Steven, are you saying that Nancy was carrying less than a million dollars?"

Steven nodded. "Half a million. I kept the other half."

"But why? And what if he'd held her prisoner while he counted the money? When he found out, she could have been—"

Steven held up a hand. "I knew he wouldn't hold Nancy, Carson. He couldn't. Counting a million bucks takes time, and he had only minutes. He must have figured we were tailing her."

"Yes, I guess you're right." Calmed, her father sat down again. "That means you'll be getting an angry call pretty soon."

"I hope so."

"I think you will," Nancy said, shifting in her chair. She was shaken too, but she was also glad about the news. "My guess is that this guy is greedy. Half a million won't be enough for him."

Nancy was right. Fifteen minutes later the phone rang. It was the extortionist. When her father put the call through the speakerphone on his desk, the voice that filled the room was electronically distorted. But there was no mistaking his anger.

"This isn't enough money, you idiot. I'll have to sell your program."

"I don't think you will," Steven said, pressing the talk button. "If you were planning to do that, why did you call?"

There was a pause.

"I want the other half-million," the voice finally said.

"Fine. But next time we make an exchange. You have to produce the program."

A burst of static came over the line. Then, "You'll hear from me."

Click. Buzzzzzz.

That was it. Nancy sat back in her chair and slowly let out her breath. How had he known to phone her father? she wondered again. Had he tried Steven's home first?

There was no way to know. For now, the extortionist still had the upper hand. At least there was one positive side to the situation, though—a second payoff meant a second chance to catch the guy.

The next morning Nancy returned to the velodrome to try to protect George. After her midnight swim with the shark, it was almost a relief. Almost.

As she parked her car, Nancy mulled over the suspects. There were only two people who had reasons to want George out of the way. Of the two, Monique Vandervoort was the stronger possibility. The KGB was ruthless, of course, but Nancy doubted they would resort to murder just to keep George and Tatyana from talking.

Inside the velodrome, it was relatively quiet. There were no spectators in the stands that day because the track portion of the Classic was over. The remaining races would all be held on the Summitville roads.

There were still plenty of cyclists training on the track, however—including George. Coming off the track for a break, she handed her bike to Nancy and wiped her forehead.

"Whew, it's hot. I'm going to the tent for a drink. Want one?"

"No," Nancy said. "But I do want to go with you. Remember what happened the last time you went to the tent by yourself?"

George laughed. "Relax. There are plenty of people hanging around outside. I won't get into any trouble, honest."

Reluctantly, Nancy let her go. She didn't want to, but she also didn't want to treat George like a baby.

A minute later Jon approached Nancy. "Can I talk to you for a minute?" he asked.

"Sure, what's up?"

"It's George. Or, rather, George and me. She

won't talk to me, Nancy. I mean, we discuss her training just as always, but when it comes to discussing us, it's like I suddenly grew a second head."

Nancy felt sorry for him. From the look in his eyes, he was really suffering. But what could she tell him?

"Look, George is hurt," she said finally, shading her eyes with her hand. "She thinks you've betrayed her."

Jon groaned. "I know. I've tried to tell her that there was nothing to it, but—"

"Was there? Nothing to it, I mean?"

"Of course. As I said, Debbi and I just talked."

"Then why do you look so guilty whenever Debbi's name comes up?"

"I—" He stopped. "I guess it shows, doesn't it?"

"Um-hmm," Nancy said.

He laughed hollowly. "You're right. I do feel guilty." He paused, but then finally the confession tumbled out of him in a rush. "The truth is, I didn't go out with Debbi just to get rid of her."

"Oh?"

"I went out with her—well, there was a time when I found her very attractive, and I wanted to see if there was still something there. You know, if maybe I had made a mistake by leaving her behind the way I did."

"And had you?"

He laughed. "No way! That's the thing. That

night I remembered all the reasons why I never wanted to get back together with her. Debbi's pretty, all right, but she's too possessive. In fact, we had only been together half an hour when she started in on all that junk about us getting married."

"Hmm—" Running her hand through her hair, Nancy gave Jon the only advice she could think of. "Why not tell George exactly what you just told me?"

"You mean tell her the truth about that night with Debbi? She'll never even *look* at me again if I do that!"

Nancy shrugged. "Maybe, maybe not. But things couldn't get much worse, could they?"

"Well, no," Jon said. "The way things are, I'm miserable. I love George. She's the best thing that's ever happened to me."

Their conversation was interrupted by a commotion near the exit tunnel. People were running toward it.

"I wonder what's going on," Jon said, squinting.

Nancy's heart began to race. "I'm not sure, but I have an awful feeling that George is involved. I'll check it out."

Handing George's bike to Jon, Nancy started to run.

Chapter Thirteen

OUTSIDE, NANCY SAW that she was right. Someone had let the guard dogs out of their cages—and they had George backed up against a chain-link fence!

"Nancy, help! Call them off!" George called.

Nancy bit her lip. She couldn't call them off. She didn't know how.

The two dogs weren't going to back off on their own, either; that much was clear. The second George moved even an inch, they growled ferociously and bared their teeth. They were ready to attack her at any moment.

What was she going to do? Turning, Nancy

looked at the small crowd of cyclists and coaches that had gathered behind her, but no one spoke up.

Just then, Debbi Howe showed up. "Ooh, poor George. What a shame."

"Debbi, this is no time to gloat. George could be mauled," Nancy said. "Call them off."

"Yeah, I guess you're right." Suddenly, Debbi stepped forward and clapped her hands twice. "Ho! Back!" she shouted.

The dogs didn't move.

"Ho! Back!" she commanded again, clapping her hands once more.

The second time it worked. Magically, the dogs turned and walked off. One was still eyeing George suspiciously, but Debbi said, "Good dog. Stay now. Stay now. Okay, George. You can move."

A minute later Nancy examined the area around the guard dogs' cages. George's windbreaker was on the ground nearby. That explained how the dogs had been given her scent, but who had let them loose in the first place?

"It wasn't me, if that's what you're thinking," Debbi said, reading Nancy's mind.

"No?"

"No. I don't have anything against George anymore," she said.

Nancy couldn't believe her ears.

"Why should I? Now that she and Jon have

broken up, Jon and I will be getting back together. Just wait and see."

From her talk with Jon, Nancy knew that Debbi was wrong. Still, she was grateful Debbi had appeared when she had. If she hadn't, George might have ended the morning hurt.

That still left the question of who had set the dogs free, however. Scanning the crowd, Nancy looked for familiar faces.

She spotted one right away—Tatyana's coach. The woman was standing on the fringe of the crowd, but it was obvious that she was very interested in the proceedings. Seeing that Nancy had spotted her, she walked over, smiling coldly.

"Once again, your friend is safe. She is very lucky."

"Yes, she is."

"Too lucky, I think. Someone with so much luck will get hurt sooner or later."

"Really?"

"Perhaps. I hope Miss Fayne will avoid getting hurt, of course. We in the Soviet Union wish only happiness to our American friends."

"How nice."

Nancy didn't believe a word of it. To her, the woman's words sounded like a veiled threat. Wanting to learn more, she decided to ask the woman a dangerous question.

"How is Tatyana doing?"

"That is none of your concern," the woman

barked. "Please tell Miss Fayne the same. We do not wish to see her interfering with Tatyana's cycling anymore."

"Oh? Has George been 'interfering' again?"

"No, but if she does—"

"Then what?" Nancy asked.

"Let us only say that her luck may not always be so good."

That was all Nancy needed to hear. As far as she was concerned, the Russians were still active suspects on her list. Monique was number one, but Tatyana's coach was running a close second.

That afternoon the first of the Classic's road events was to be held on Route 133, a flat, straight state highway that ran through Summitville. In the event, the cyclists would race against the clock over a fixed distance.

The Women's Time Trial was won by a French rider, Sandrine Dubois. George placed third, but she wasn't too unhappy. "I'm still first in the overall standings," she pointed out.

As they watched the men begin their time trial, Nancy wondered whether George was as lucky as she thought she was. Someone was still trying to kill her, and if Nancy was right about the would-be murderer's identity, as long as George held her lead in the standings she was only putting herself in greater danger.

* * *

Later the girls were standing in the velodrome parking lot, each balancing one of George's bikes.

"Nice bike," a man said, nodding toward the disk-wheel bike.

"Thanks," George answered.

The man put his hand in his pocket and nervously jingled some coins. "How much does a bike like that go for?"

George shrugged. "I'm not really sure. Several thousand, I think."

"Yeah? How would you like to sell that one to me? I'll give you five thousand."

George stared at him in surprise. "Excuse me?"

"I said I'll give you five thousand dollars for your bike," the man said, lowering his voice. "How does that sound?"

Nancy could hardly believe what she was hearing. Obviously, neither could George. For a second there was dead silence.

"That's a generous offer. Tell me, do you want the derailleurs and cranks with that, or do you have your own?" George asked.

"Huh?" The man looked confused. "What are you talking about?"

"Don't you know?"

"Uh—"

"I didn't think so. You don't know beans about bikes. So what's going on here? Why are you trying to buy my bike from me?"

"Look, I'll make it six—cash." Reaching into the pocket of his jacket, the man pulled out a wad of crisp, new hundred-dollar bills.

George had had enough. "I'm sorry, the bike is not for sale."

"Come on, this is a great deal. Six thousand, okay?"

"I said forget it."

Defeated, the man quickly walked away. When he was gone, Nancy and George exchanged puzzled looks.

"That was *weird,"* Nancy said.

"You're telling me," George said. "That guy didn't even know what a derailleur is! Everyone who knows anything about bikes knows that."

Nancy was curious about the incident, too. But all conversation in the area came to a sudden halt as a piercing scream cut the air!

Chapter Fourteen

NANCY LOOKED AROUND. She couldn't tell where the scream had come from. All she could see were rows of cars, cyclists, and spectators. Now everyone was glancing around.

Then the scream split the air again. That time Nancy could tell it was coming from somewhere to her right. Handing her bike to George, she jogged in that direction to search the rows of cars. A minute later she found the problem.

It was Monique. The Dutch cyclist, still wearing her orange jersey and black cycling shorts, was backed against the side of a car. She was hysterical with fear. A dog was barking ferociously at her. The look on Monique's face was exactly the same as the one that had been on George's earlier, but this time Nancy wanted to laugh.

The dog that had cornered Monique was a poodle!

Within seconds Nancy was joined by a small crowd. At first, no one seemed to understand what the problem was. Then they got a demonstration.

"Yip! Yip! Yip!" the poodle barked.

"Aaah. G-get it away! H-help! Get it away from me!" Monique cried.

Moments later the poodle's owner, the mother of a cyclist, ran up. At the same time, a tall blond man wearing a cycling cap and a sweat suit that matched Monique's jersey ran over too. Her coach, Nancy guessed.

"Oh, I'm so very sorry," the owner of the poodle said as she scooped the dog up in her arms. "Tiger here got away from me."

"G-get it away from me! Please!" Monique gasped.

"Please remove the dog," the girl's coach requested.

"Of course. I'm so very sorry," the woman repeated. "Bad Tiger! Bad dog!" she scolded, hurrying away.

Nancy shook her head in bewilderment. The whole thing was ridiculous. How could a tough, aggressive competitor like Monique be frightened by a poodle?

Monique's coach put an arm around her and

said something to her in Dutch. Then, for the benefit of the bystanders, he explained in English, "Since she was a little girl, she has had a fear of dogs. Thank you for helping."

Nancy turned away with the others and started back to George. That answered her question —and also eliminated another suspect. If Monique were afraid of dogs, she couldn't have been the one who turned the velodrome guard dogs on George. And that meant the culprit had to be the deadliest suspect of all—the KGB.

That evening Nancy was invited to dinner at the Faynes'. Bess and Ned were invited, too. Everyone lounged on the deck in the backyard while Mr. Fayne grilled hamburgers. As they waited, Nancy looked around.

It was a beautiful night. Still, she couldn't forget the danger George was in. It was quite possible that she was a target of the Soviet secret service. Even now, the KGB agents could be plotting their next attack.

Nancy knew she had to convince George of the danger. But how? Would George believe it?

Nancy's opportunity came after dinner as they carried the dishes into the kitchen. "George, do you have a minute?" she asked.

"Sure, Nan. What's up?"

"I feel like walking off some of that food. Want to go with me?"

"All right. I'm feeling pretty stuffed myself," George said.

Together they walked around the side of the house, down the driveway, and out onto the sidewalk. They began to stroll down the street. It was growing dark, and lights were already coming on inside the houses.

"Is there something special on your mind, Nancy?" George asked.

Slowly, Nancy ran down the facts in the case. One by one she described the attacks and discussed the suspects. Finally, she laid out her conclusion: the KGB was after George.

When she was finished, George shrugged. "I kind of figured that was it. But so what? What can I do about it?"

"Drop out of the Classic."

"Oh no. Not that again."

"George, it's the only way. They're ruthless and they're gunning for you. Your good luck won't last forever."

George walked in silence for a minute, her hands jammed in the back pockets of her jeans. When she spoke, her voice was full of disappointment. Her words were bitter. "You know, of all my friends I thought you were the one who'd understand. Bess—well, I expected her reaction. But not you. Nancy, you love sports as much as I do."

"I also like being alive."

Suddenly George stopped. "Do you think I don't?" she said explosively. "For the last five days I've been terrified!"

"You have?"

"Sure! Do you think I enjoy breathing smoke, swimming in electrified pools, and everything else? No way!"

Nancy was surprised. All week George had been so brave. Whenever she'd mentioned the attacks, it had been in a joking way. Not once had she showed her fear.

"Then quit the Classic," Nancy said again.

"I can't. I don't want to." George was adamant. "Anyway, there's only one event left—the 40-Kilometer Road Race tomorrow."

Nancy put her hands on her hips. "I don't see why that's so important. What harm would it do to skip the last event?"

"You don't understand. You don't have any idea how important this is to me, do you?"

Nancy tried to calm down. "Look, if you won't drop out of the race, then at least stop talking to Tatyana. Stay away from her tomorrow. Brush her off."

"No," George insisted. "I won't do that either."

"George, please!"

"It's a matter of principle. No government has the right to put limits on a friendship. What they're doing is wrong."

Nancy threw up her hands. There was nothing

more she could say, nothing more to do. George was determined to keep going, and that was all there was to it.

"Oh, Nan, don't be like that," George pleaded. "I need your help right now."

"Why? So I can get Bess and your parents off your back about dropping out?"

"No, that's not it at all."

"What do you mean?" Nancy asked. "What is it, then?"

Turning, George started walking back in the direction of her house. "It's—it's Jon. I miss him so much, Nancy."

She wasn't surprised. "I can imagine. But what can *I* do?"

"Help me get my feelings straightened out. I'm so confused!"

All the way back to George's house, they talked. Gradually, Nancy's anger lessened. The more she heard, the more she realized that George was hurting badly. Finally, she said, "Why don't you just forgive him?"

"I'm trying," George replied. "But it's hard."

"Don't you believe his story about the night he was out with Debbi?"

"Sure. What bothers me is that he wasn't honest about it."

That was true. He hadn't told her the whole truth at first. "Why don't you talk to him about it?" Nancy suggested.

"What for? There's nothing else to say!"

Biting her lower lip, Nancy thought back to her discussion with Jon. There was a lot more to say.

"Listen, George, I can't tell you how to handle this, but I can tell you one thing—Jon loves you as much as you love him. It's crazy for you to be apart."

"So what should I do?"

"Talk. Work it out. No relationship is perfect."

"But what if we can't work it out? Nancy, I'll die!"

"Seems to me you're in pretty bad shape already."

"Yeah. If the KGB doesn't get me, a broken heart will."

Nancy laughed, but the laughter didn't make her feel better. In a way, George's words were all too true.

Chapter Fifteen

THE NEXT DAY was gray and overcast. Nancy parked her Mustang in the center of Summitville and walked to the starting line for the 40-Kilometer Road Race. It was the last day of the Summitville Junior Classic. It could also be the last day of George's life, but Nancy was determined to see that it wasn't.

At the starting area, she found Jon. Ned and Bess were there too, having driven to Summitville in their own cars.

"Where's George?" she asked.

"Down the road warming up," Jon replied.

A faint ray of hope touched Nancy. "Do you

think there's any way you could persuade her to drop out?"

"Yeah. After all, you're her coach," Ned said.

"I could give it a try," Jon said. "I don't think it'll do any good, but what do I have to lose?"

A short while later George came back from her warm-up ride. Seeing Jon standing with Nancy and the others, she pointedly rode past them without a word and stopped instead by the starting line. She began talking to Tatyana.

Bad move, Nancy thought angrily. Tatyana's coaches were standing not ten feet away, watching her! Didn't George realize?

Jon went over to George and spoke to her for almost five minutes. Nancy saw him gesturing with his hands and pounding one fist into his other palm. George listened, saying nothing. When Jon was finished, she shook her head and rode away.

"It's no use. She won't drop out," Jon reported.

Nancy's heart sank. "That's it, then. We'll have to put our contingency plan into action. Did you bring the equipment, Ned?"

Ned lifted his knapsack. "Got it right here."

"Good. Let's get moving."

Twenty minutes later an announcement over the loudspeaker called all the women to the starting line. Nancy and Ned were already there.

Ned was in the backseat of the official car that would ride ahead of the cyclists. Nancy was in a support van that would ride behind them.

Pulling up the antenna of the walkie-talkie she was holding, Nancy punched the talk button. "Ned, can you hear me?"

Static crackled, then she heard Ned's voice. "Loud and clear."

"Great. I'm beginning to think this will work. The two of us should be able to keep George in sight all the way through the race."

"Let's hope so," Ned replied. "I'll check in again after the start."

Nancy smiled. Having Ned's help made her feel much better. She was glad she'd called him up the previous night, too. Between them they had come up with a plan to protect George until the Classic was over. Then Nancy had made the arrangements with the race officials while Ned rented the walkie-talkies.

Leaning forward in her seat, Nancy looked out the window. "Hey, it just hit me. George is riding her old bike. In fact, now that I think of it, she rode it yesterday. How come?"

"Disk wheels don't accelerate fast enough for road racing," Jon explained. He was driving the van. "They can be a problem if there's any wind. You get blown across the road."

"They act sort of like sails, huh?"

"That's right."

"You know, George really chose a great place to hide her disk-wheel bike. I suppose she put it there now, too," Nancy said.

Jon chuckled. "Yeah. She's pretty clever. And you can bet it's there now."

Nancy smiled. Hiding the bike in plain sight was a great way to confuse potential thieves. Just then Nancy's thoughts were cut short. Prerace instructions were being given to the riders over the loudspeaker.

A few minutes later the race began. The course was ten kilometers long, and it started in the center of town. It cut through a housing development, went up a mile-long grade, swung through the state park, then wound back into town. The riders would go around four times.

"Watch for attacks on that long uphill grade," Jon said as they started off.

"Attacks?" Nancy asked in alarm.

He shook his head. "Not the kind you're thinking of. I'm talking about breakaway attempts. The main strategy in a road race is to break away with a small group. Then you can draft with them, and when you get to the sprint at the end of the race you won't have so much competition."

"The sprint?" Nancy stared at him in amazement. "Are you telling me that after racing forty kilometers, they actually *sprint* to the finish?"

Jon smiled. "You got it. Cycling isn't a sport for slackers."

"I guess not!"

Ahead of her, Nancy had a perfect view. At the front of the race there was a police motorcycle, followed by the official lead car, where Ned was. After that came the racers. Behind them were more motorcycles, plus support vehicles like the one she was in. A few had spare wheels—and even spare frames—on their roofs.

About halfway through the first lap, Nancy's radio squawked. "How's it look back there?" Ned asked.

"So far so good," Nancy replied.

"Maybe we were worried about nothing."

"I sure hope so, but let's wait and see. It isn't over yet."

The racers tore down an incline, moving toward the town. In practically no time, they were back in the center of Summitville, zooming under the overhead banner at the start-finish line.

"Three more laps to go," Jon said. "Not much action so far."

There wasn't much action on the second lap, either. On the third, however, there was a dramatic breakaway at the beginning of the long uphill grade. "There they go!" Jon said.

"Where's George?" Nancy asked. She couldn't pick out her friend.

"She's stuck in the middle of the pack," Jon announced. "Too bad. That break looks strong.

By the time they hit the park, they're going to be half a mile ahead."

Jon was right. As Nancy watched, the gap between the breakaway riders and the field widened. A short while later, they were almost out of sight—and so was Ned.

The radio squawked. "Hope you've still got George in sight," Ned said.

"Roger. I can see her clearly now. She's moving up to the head of the field."

"That's good, because I—"

"Wait a minute! George is breaking away!" Nancy said, interrupting him.

"Solo?"

"Yes. She's about fifty yards ahead of the field—sixty maybe. Can you see her?"

"No. We just came into the forest. All I can see are the lead riders."

"Keep an eye out for her. At the rate she's going, she should catch the breakaway group in a few minutes."

"Let's hope so," Ned said anxiously.

Nancy released the talk button. Her heart was pounding.

Jon whistled softly. "That's a gutsy move George is making."

Nancy swallowed nervously. "If she makes it."

Jon nodded. "She's a strong rider, but we'll have to wait and see."

Nancy found Jon's words ironic—she could

barely see George at all. Then Nancy lost sight of her altogether.

"Ned, have you got George in sight yet?"

"Negative." Ned's voice was tense. "The break is picking up speed. She'll have to work hard to catch up."

For the next few minutes, Nancy waited nervously for word from Ned. It never came. Ahead of her, a police motorcycle left the support caravan, roared around the cyclists, and took off. What was going on? And why wasn't the rider in uniform?

Finally, they were back in the center of Summitville again.

"Do you see George yet?" Nancy asked Ned.

"Negative," the reply came back. "I guess she's still halfway between us."

Just then, the van crossed the start-finish line. "One more lap to go," Jon said.

The next few minutes were agonizing. Ahead of Nancy, the field stayed together. There were no more breakaways. From Ned she learned that the leading breakaway was still intact, but George had not caught up to it. George was riding the last two laps solo! She had to be working very hard.

Finally, Nancy heard from Ned. "The breakaway just crossed the finish line," he reported.

"Thanks."

Nancy's van crossed the line a few minutes later. As soon as they'd parked, she hopped out and went to find George. After a few minutes of looking, however, she still hadn't found her. "Where is she?" she asked Ned when they met up.

"I don't know. Wait, there are Bess and Jon. Maybe they can tell us."

But they hadn't seen George, either. Bess hadn't even seen her cross the finish line.

"Then what happened to her?" Ned asked.

Jon looked puzzled. "She wasn't in the break, and she wasn't with the field."

"She didn't finish in between them, either," Bess said.

Nancy had a hollow feeling in the pit of her stomach. She didn't want to believe it, but it was true—George had vanished!

Chapter Sixteen

NANCY IMMEDIATELY BEGAN to organize a search. Going back along the route, they questioned all the spectators. Everyone said they'd seen George go by in the third lap, but no one had seen her during the fourth.

Nancy wasn't sure that they'd ever see her again. But there was no point in telling anyone that. Having sent the others out to search, Nancy got into her car to hold a hurried conference with Ned. There were two possibilities to consider. Either George had been killed on the course, or she'd been kidnapped.

"The first possibility's out," Ned said reasonably.

"I agree." Nancy nodded. "If George was killed on the course, we'd know about it already."

"That leaves kidnapping, and that means we may still have time to save her. But how are we going to track her down?"

"I don't know. I don't even know where to start!" Nancy said.

Then she remembered the motorcycle that had roared away from the support caravan. She grabbed Ned's arm.

"Ned! When George broke away from the field and was riding so low, a motorcycle took off after her!"

"A policeman?"

"Yes, but it wasn't a regular motorcycle cop. The driver wasn't wearing a uniform."

"All right! That's the first decent clue we've had," Ned said excitedly. "He could be our man. And if that's true, maybe he forced George down a side street."

"To a getaway car? That's possible, but in that case someone would have seen them, right? It would have been reported."

Ned drummed his fingers on the dashboard. "Maybe, but maybe not. It could have happened somewhere where no one was around."

"True."

"And if we can find that place, we may be able to pick up some clues."

"Let's go."

Nancy started the car, and a minute later they were circling the course. They both looked right and left for deserted side streets.

"Ned, look! Over there—near that big tree stump."

"Nancy, that's just a path," Ned said. "A car couldn't get down there."

"No, but a motorcycle could. Let's check it out."

Nancy slammed her own car into reverse, then backed into the path's entrance. The Mustang fit but not by much. Branches scraped the car's rear window.

Nancy opened her door and got out. "Come on, let's see if we can find anything!"

The ground was dry, so there were no tire tracks to be seen. And there were no broken twigs or branches to indicate that a car had passed by recently.

They walked into the woods for about a quarter of a mile. Nothing. Ned thought it was a waste of time, but Nancy pushed on. She was certain that the trail would give them a clue to George's whereabouts. Besides, it was the only lead they had.

Then, two hundred yards later, Nancy suddenly stopped.

"Ned!" She grabbed his arm. Sticking out from the bushes ahead of them was the rear wheel of George's road bike! Its tire was flat, and its spokes were bent.

They ran up and pulled it out onto the path. As they did, Nancy spotted George. Her friend lay in a crumpled heap in the bushes, a large gash on the side of her head. She was breathing, Nancy saw, but she was unconscious.

As they pulled her out, Nancy silently vowed that she would find the people responsible for this and bring them to justice—no matter what!

An hour later Nancy sat in the emergency room at River Heights Hospital, waiting for a report from the doctors. She felt awful. She'd expected an attack from the side of the road, but why hadn't she seen that anyone could just force George off the course?

Finally, a doctor in a surgical gown came into the room. George's parents jumped up from their chairs. Nancy, Ned, Jon, and Bess crowded around, too.

"Doctor, what happened?" Mrs. Fayne asked.

"Is she going to be okay?" Jon questioned.

The doctor held up his hands. "One at a time. First, George is going to be fine. As for what happened, it appears that she was hit on the head with a heavy object."

"Is she awake?" Mrs. Fayne asked.

"No, she's still unconscious and probably will be for some time."

Jon groaned.

Mr. Fayne stepped forward. "Doctor, will there be any permanent damage?"

"It's too soon to say. She almost certainly has a concussion, but we won't know how bad it is until we see the X rays."

Nancy said goodbye to the others and quickly ran out to her car. She had to take some action. The time for sitting and contemplating was long past.

Nancy turned into the parking lot of the Imperial Motel. A light rain was falling. All over the courtyard, cyclists and their crews were packing cars, dashing back and forth from their rooms.

Nancy parked and switched off the engine, but she kept the windshield wipers going. Twenty yards away, the Soviet coach was standing in the door of Tatyana's room, supervising the loading. Tatyana came out, carrying a suitcase.

At the sight of her, Nancy's anger rose to the breaking point. It wasn't fair, she thought. All George had wanted was to get to know Tatyana, a fellow cyclist. For that, she'd been subjected to several murder attempts and a visit to the hospital. Worse, the culprits were now getting away, and there was nothing Nancy could do with no evidence.

Chapter Seventeen

NANCY HEADED HOME, her mind in turmoil. She owed it to George to apprehend her attacker. But where were the necessary clues and evidence?

Her frustration mounted when she arrived home. Turning into her driveway, she saw that Steven Lloyd's car was there. Great, she thought. On top of everything else, she had to tell him that his protégée was hospitalized.

To her surprise, Steven wasn't overly upset. In fact, once he was sure that George would be okay, he seemed to forget about her. He was preoccupied with his own troubles—the extortionist still hadn't called back. What was holding him up? When would the program be returned?

"I tell you, Carson, this thing is driving me crazy," he said. The three of them were sitting in Nancy's father's study. "If I don't get that program back, and soon, it may not be worth anything. The thief may have sold it to someone already."

The anguish in his voice was obvious, but Nancy didn't know what to say. "If it helps any," she told him, "I'll be glad to make the next drop-off. As long as it doesn't involve sharks!"

Steven smiled. "Thanks, but this time I intend to make the drop-off myself. I want to be sure I get my hands on the program."

"You will." Nancy's father tried to console him. "Just hang on."

Not long after that, the phone rang. It was the extortionist.

"What's been keeping you?" Steven asked, angrily jabbing the talk button on the speakerphone.

"Patience, Mr. Lloyd," the electronic voice said. "There was a little problem on this end, but now it's been cleared up. I'll be ready to exchange your program for the money shortly. Stay by the telephone." *Click. Buzzzzz . . .*

The three of them stared at the speakerphone.

"I wish I could figure out how he knows to call here," her father said. "Did you tell anyone you were coming over?"

Steven shook his head. "No, it's the same as before. I only wrote it down on my calendar."

"Hmm," Carson Drew mumbled, shaking his head. Then he shrugged. "Shall we go see if Hannah's got dinner ready?"

"Sure. I hope she won't be insulted if I don't eat much. I'm really not hungry," Steven said.

Nancy wasn't hungry, either. Hannah had fixed corn chowder and sandwiches, but Nancy barely touched the food. Finally, after staring at her plate long enough, Nancy excused herself and went out to her car. Evening visiting hours at the hospital would end soon, and she wanted to check on her friend.

Twisting her car through the streets, Nancy thought about the case from every angle. Was it the KGB who had tried to kill George? And if it was, why, after so many attempts, hadn't they succeeded? Why had they merely knocked her out and dumped her in the woods?

It didn't make sense.

Unless it wasn't the KGB at all. What if it was . . .

Suddenly Nancy slammed on the brakes. Excitement raced through her. She had it! Of course! Why hadn't she seen it sooner? All along, she'd been asking herself the wrong question. The issue wasn't *why* someone was trying to kill George but *whether* they were trying to kill her at all!

And if they weren't, that meant—

Nancy pulled over to the side of the road and sat for a few minutes, working out the details in her head. Yes, all the pieces of the puzzle fit perfectly. The note—the pool—the car window—even the shark!

There was just one problem. She had to move fast. The culprit would be making his getaway—and soon!

Chapter Eighteen

SHIFTING INTO GEAR again, Nancy drove to the nearest phone booth and called Ned at his house. Quickly, she explained the facts. "Meet me at the velodrome as fast as you can, okay? Oh, and Ned?"

"Yes?"

"Call my father. He'll want to know what's going on."

She hung up, raced back to her car, and took off. The velodrome wasn't far away, but it was important for her to get there as fast as she could.

When she arrived, Nancy swung into the parking lot. It was empty. Slamming her door, she raced to the entrance gate. It was open, so she went right in.

She raced through the entrance tunnel. Inside, the track and infield were illuminated by several floodlights. Quickly she went to the raised judges' platform in the middle of the infield. Its underside was masked by a canvas curtain. She pulled it aside.

Good. George's bike was still there, chained to a support post. It was a strange place to hide it, but clever. Nancy couldn't understand how George could put it in such an obvious spot without anyone seeing her take it out or put it back. Apparently, though, no one did. The bike was safer there than it would be in her own garage.

Nancy was about to leave the infield when she heard footsteps echoing in the exit tunnel. It had to be George's attacker. Nancy needed to hide. Facing him now wasn't part of her plan.

Ducking under the judges' platform, she crouched next to the bike and waited. Several minutes passed. She heard scraping sounds nearby, and then there was silence. Then footsteps crunched slowly on the gravel around the platform. Nancy's heart began to hammer like a drum. Suddenly the canvas was ripped roughly aside.

"You! What are you doing under there?" Peter Cooper growled when he saw Nancy.

"Resting?" Nancy answered.

"What?"

"Well, it was raining, and—"

"Never mind. Get out of there!"

Nancy crawled out from under the platform and stood up. Peter was holding a large chain cutter in his hand. At his feet was a bulging duffel bag. He was obviously packed for a trip.

Nancy was torn. Part of her wanted to run, and part of her wanted to stall. Facing him without a backup was a bad idea, but she really didn't have a choice.

She decided to stall. It wouldn't take Ned long to arrive, and while she waited she could try for a confession.

"So, how's the extortion business these days?" she asked mildly.

"Extortion? What are you talking about?" Peter replied coldly.

"I should have figured out what was going on when I went to Steven's office with my father," she said.

Peter dropped the chain cutter and folded his arms. "You're not making a lot of sense, Nancy," he said, looking at her severely.

"Oh, no? Well, I'll explain. It starts with the password to Steven's program. Passwords are very hard to guess, and even with a code-busting program you have to work for hours. I think you did crack it eventually, though—on the night you put George's bike together in Steven's office."

"Really?"

"Yes, but something must have gone wrong with your plan," Nancy went on. "Maybe Steven came down the hall just after you'd copied his program and deleted it from his disk. Anyway, you had to hide your copy, and you did—inside one of George's disk wheels."

Peter shook his head. "That's an amusing story, Nancy, but you're forgetting something. Everyone knows that program was stolen on the night *after* George got her bike."

"No, it wasn't. You just made it look that way when you went back the following night, turned off the alarm system, and smashed down Steven's door."

"I did all that, did I?" He looked unconcerned.

Nancy plunged on. "Yes, you did all that. We figured it couldn't be an inside job, because it looked so professional. In reality, though, it was both—inside *and* professional."

"You've concocted quite a scenario, Nancy," he said. "But that's all it is—a scenario. You have no proof. If you go to the police, they'll say your imagination is working overtime. They'll say you're upset about your friend."

"George. Oh yes, I almost forgot about George," Nancy said. "That's the part that stumped me the most. All week I thought someone was trying to kill her, but I was wrong."

"Oh?"

Nancy was getting angry now. "You weren't trying to kill her—not deliberately. All you wanted was to get your hands on her bike."

Peter laughed harshly. "Now you really sound crazy."

"Was I crazy when you tried to take the bike on the first day of the Classic? You remember —when George complained that the seat needed to be adjusted?"

"No, but so what?"

"Well, you weren't able to get the bike that time because Jon fixed the seat. So later you tried to get it by creating a diversion. You set the tent on fire, with George inside."

"That's ridiculous."

"Is it? I don't think so. I think you were foiled because Bess stayed inside the velodrome to guard the bike. Later that afternoon, you tried again at the Imperial Motel."

Peter said nothing.

"The whole week went by like that," Nancy said, her fury rising. "Time after time you tried to get the bike. Like at Big Top Burgers or with the guard dogs—it didn't matter. You needed that bike, and you needed it bad.

"Finally," she said, "George found a new place to hide the bike. You searched her house that night but found nothing. It wasn't there. Then you decided to force the location out of her—which you did this morning. Afterward, you hit her on the head with a rock and left her in the woods."

"That's enough," Peter barked. His mouth was drawn in a tight line. "You think you're so smart. You think you've got it all worked out, but tell me this—how are you going to prove it?"

"Simple. I'm going to take the wheels off that bike."

"Don't make me laugh. You don't know that there's anything in there."

"No?" Nancy glanced at the chain cutters. "Then what are *you* doing here?"

Suddenly, Peter lunged. The bluffing was over. Nancy dodged out of his way, but before she could run two steps he tripped her. When she looked up from the ground, Peter's duffel bag was unzipped. He was standing over her with a revolver in his hand.

He grabbed her roughly by the arm. "Why did you have to poke your nose into it, huh? I ought to—"

He jerked her roughly to her feet. She wanted to scream but didn't. The next second he pulled her close to him and pressed the cold barrel of the revolver deep into her cheek.

"Let me go!"

"No way, Detective Drew. You're never going to tell anyone what you know."

"What are you going to do?" she asked. "Feed me to the shark again?"

He laughed coldly. "Too bad it didn't finish

you off that night. This time I'll find a better way to get you out of my way. But first—"

He shoved her to the ground. Nancy landed hard and felt the wind being knocked out of her. She gasped, trying to catch her breath. As she did, Peter quickly cut through the chain on the bike and pulled it into the open.

Pointing the gun at her again, he kicked his duffel bag. "Pick it up. We're going for a ride in my car."

Nancy knew where that ride would end—on a dead-end road. She had to escape, now! Where was Ned, anyway?

Bending down, she grabbed the handles of the duffel bag. She couldn't wait for help anymore. She would have to help herself. Lifting the bag, she threw it straight at Peter. It caught him in the chest.

"Ooof!"

He went over, and the bike toppled to the ground, too. The gun landed ten feet away. Nancy ran and grabbed the bike, her heart in her throat. Hopping on it, she started for the exit tunnel. She had to get out of there with the evidence!

Pedaling the bike turned out to be harder than she thought. The wheels were heavy, and building up speed took time. She didn't need much motivation, though, and within seconds she was speeding toward the tunnel entrance. Then she gasped.

The entrance was blocked! Peter had dragged several police barriers in front of it. Why hadn't she gone for the pistol instead? she thought desperately. By now, Peter had picked it up and was coming after her. What was she going to do?

Chapter Nineteen

THERE WAS ONLY one choice. Pedaling harder than before, Nancy changed direction and rode onto the track.

Standing up on the pedals, Nancy rode faster and faster. She was a perfect target, and that scared her. The only thing in her favor was that she was moving. Realizing that, she began to weave back and forth. It wasn't a big advantage, but at least it was something.

Pow! A concrete chip flew off the track in front of her.

Pow! Another chip flew up right below her feet.

Nancy's heart hammered. She pedaled harder.

Her only hope was to keep going. She was a duck in a shooting gallery, but if she could just stay alive until Ned arrived . . .

Then she hit the first banked turn. It was like taking a banked turn in a car, but a lot more immediate. The slightest turn of the handlebars sent her flashing up the incline, and the slightest tilt of her body sent her racing back down.

In no time she was off it, speeding down the back straight.

Pow! Pow! More concrete chips flew.

He had not hit her yet, but Nancy knew it was just a matter of time.

Pow!

Hunching down, she pedaled even harder. Her legs were aching. Her lungs were burning, ready to explode.

Nancy knew that she couldn't go on much longer. She had to do something—anything! She was coming out of a turn. Maybe she could . . .

There was no time to think it through. Just do it! she told herself.

She swung off the track. The bike rattled as she rode over the apron, over the gravel, and went streaking across the infield.

Ahead of her, Peter raised his gun and steadied it. His hand jerked. *Pow!*

Nancy swerved to the right, then the left. She was thirty yards away—twenty—

Pow! Pow!

Fifteen—ten. Now she could see his face, his surprise and alarm. He started to run, but she steered toward him. Seconds later, she ran him down.

Wham!

Nancy hit the ground like a sack, but she was up again in a flash. On the ground, ten feet away, was the pistol. She dove for it, grabbed it, and staggered to her feet.

"Freeze, Peter!"

Peter froze in a half crouch, staring at the gun pointed at his heart. "I don't believe—"

"Believe it! Make one move and you're history!" Nancy panted.

"Nancy?"

A familiar voice echoed behind her. A second later Ned ran in with a dozen policemen. All of whom had their pistols drawn.

She was safe! Flinging Peter's pistol as far as she could, Nancy collapsed.

Peter Cooper was led away in handcuffs. When Nancy finished telling her story to the police, she joined her father and Steven Lloyd. They were on the apron of the track, taking apart the disk-wheel bike.

"Easy, Carson, slowly—slowly. There. That's it."

As Nancy walked up, her father separated the two halves of the front wheel. Inside was a floppy disk, the hubset fitted through its center hole.

She'd been right after all. And this evidence would send Peter to jail.

Steven turned to her with a grateful smile. "I can't thank you enough, Nancy," he said. "I've got my program back, and not only that, I've got my money back, too."

"You do?" Nancy asked, surprised.

"Yes," her father explained. "According to the police, Cooper had the half-million dollars stashed in his duffel bag."

"I'll bet it was all there except for a few thousand dollars, right?" Nancy said.

"That's true. How did you know?" her father asked.

"At the time trial yesterday morning, a man tried to buy George's bike with a pocket full of hundred-dollar bills. He didn't know anything about bicycles, though, so he must have been someone Peter paid to do it."

Carson Drew nodded. "Sounds logical. Well, knowing the identity of the villain sure makes it easier to understand things, doesn't it?"

"You said it," Steven agreed. "Like the delays in phoning the drop-off instructions. Peter didn't call because he didn't have the program to exchange for the money!"

"It also explains how he knew to phone you at our house. He peeked at your desk calendar," Carson Drew said.

"There's one thing I'm still not clear about," Nancy commented.

"What's that?" her father asked.

"Why did Peter steal the program in the first place?"

"I can answer that," Steven said. "It was greed, pure and simple. Peter was a conscientious worker, but he was also obsessed with money."

"How do you know?" Carson Drew asked.

"Well, for one thing, he frequently asked me how much money I've made. When I finally told him, he seemed resentful. I couldn't understand it at the time, but now I can see that he wanted to get rich, too."

"Yes, the easy way," Nancy remarked.

"One final question, Nancy," her father said. "What gave you the solution?"

Nancy thought for a moment. "It was George. You see, I couldn't figure out why the person who was trying to kill her hadn't finished the job when he had the chance."

"And?" he asked.

"It bothered me for hours! Then, finally, I realized that there was only one explanation. The guy hadn't killed her because he wasn't after George—he was after something else!"

"The bike."

"Right."

Ned came up to them. "Nancy, I called the hospital. George regained consciousness a few minutes ago."

"Well, it's about time!" she joked.

"Do you want to go see her?"

"You bet!" She glanced at her watch. "But we'd better hurry."

"Yeah, visiting hours will be over soon."

At the hospital, Jon and Bess were already in George's room. The nurses didn't like having so many people there at once, but they did allow it.

"So, George, looks like it really takes a lot to get you to tell where you keep your equipment hidden," Nancy said, eyeing her bandages.

George laughed, then winced. "Ow! Don't make me laugh, Nan. It hurts too much."

"Sorry."

"Yeah. Maybe next time you should just leave it out in the open where anybody can steal it," Bess said.

"Ha-ha. Ow!" George cried.

"Oops! I'm sorry!"

"Forget it. Let's talk about something that won't make me laugh, okay?"

"Okay," Ned said, leaning on the rail by her bed. "Tell me, why did you hide the bike in the first place?"

"Yeah, did you really have to be so careful?" Bess added.

"The main reason was that it wasn't my bike," George explained. "After my car was broken into, I was afraid someone would try to steal it. Which they did."

Nancy looked at Jon and smiled. His feelings for George were written all over his face. He obviously cared for her a lot, but did George know that? Had they had a chance to work things out?

A minute later she got her answer. Turning in her bed, George touched Nancy's hand. "I've got to thank you for something."

"Saving your life?"

"Yes, that, but also something else—for getting Jon and me back together. He explained all that stuff about Debbi tonight. He also told me that he wouldn't have explained if you hadn't convinced him to."

"You're not upset?" Nancy asked.

"Because he was still attracted to her? He wouldn't be human if he didn't have some pretty strong feelings about an old girlfriend," she said earnestly.

Jon overheard their conversation. "Yes, thanks, Nancy. I owe you double. Hey, George, you look kind of thirsty. Want me to get you some water or a soda or something?"

"A soda would be great."

"Okay, I'll be right back."

"I'll go with you," Ned said. "I could use one myself."

When the two were gone, Nancy, Bess, and George were alone in the room. For a minute none of them spoke.

As Nancy looked down at George in her hospital bed, she thought back over their friendship.

There were so many warm, funny, and frightening memories. Sure, she'd saved George's life on this case, but George had done the same for her many times before. Bess, too. The friendship the three of them shared went deep. It was based on a lot more than clothes, gossip, and boys—although there was plenty of that! It was based on trust. And love. George and Bess were the greatest.

But there was one thing she still didn't understand. "George, can I ask you a question?"

"Sure."

"For days we thought that someone at the velodrome was trying to kill you. But every time we asked you to drop out of the Classic, you said no. How come? Why wouldn't you quit?"

George closed her eyes. "I guess I should explain that, huh?"

"I *am* curious."

For a long minute, George said nothing. Then she reopened her eyes and glanced at them both. "It was because of you and Bess."

"What! Because of *us?*"

"The truth is, I've always admired you both so."

Bess was shocked. *"You* admire *me?"*

"Sure. Think about it. Nancy, you're so incredibly smart, and Bess, you're so incredibly pretty." George smiled. "Anyway, all I have is sports. It's the only thing I've ever been good at."

"Is that why you've always worked so hard at sports?" Nancy asked. "So you could keep up with us in a way?"

"Sort of. It's hard to explain. All I know is that the Classic was the biggest event I've ever entered. I really wanted to sweep it. Oh, how I wanted to sweep it!"

"You almost did," Bess said softly. "If you'd finished that road race—"

"I know. I would have been first in the overall standings," George said bitterly.

A wave of affection swept over Nancy. "George?"

"Yeah?"

"I think there's something you should know. You don't have to do anything special, or be anything special on account of Bess and me. Right, Bess?"

Bess nodded. "You said it. We love you just the way you are, Georgia Fayne."

Nancy's next case:

Bess Marvin is thrilled when she gets to meet her favorite heartthrob of the soaps, Rick Arlen. But Nancy isn't so delighted. Rick's been receiving death threats, and she's been recruited to protect him.

Who would want to kill a lovable TV star? Just about everybody, Nancy discovers. It could be a soap fan who doesn't like Rick's character. Or it could be an angry ex-girlfriend—Rick has lots of those. And then there are all the enemies he's made on the set.

Nancy has to work fast—Bess is quickly losing her heart to Rick. But the deeper Nancy digs, the more dangerous things get in *STAY TUNED FOR DANGER*, Case #17 in The Nancy Drew Files™.

ARMADA

All these books are available at your local bookshop or newsagent, or can be ordered from the publisher. To order direct from the publishers just tick the title you want and fill in the form below:

Name ______________________________

Address ______________________________

____

Send to: Collins Childrens Cash Sales
PO Box 11
Falmouth
Cornwall
TR10 9EN

Please enclose a cheque or postal order or debit my Visa/ Access –

Credit card no:

Expiry date:

Signature:

– to the value of the cover price plus:

UK: 60p for the first book, 25p for the second book, plus 15p per copy for each additional book ordered to a maximum charge of £1.90.

BFPO: 60p for the first book, 25p for the second book plus 15p per copy for the next 7 books, thereafter 9p per book.

Overseas and Eire: £1.25 for the first book, 75p for the second book. Thereafter 28p per book.

Armada reserve the right to show new retail prices on covers which may differ from those previously advertised in the text or elswhere.